JUMP START

CHERRY BLOSSOM POINT

CHRISTINE GAEL

D1519613

INTRODUCTION

Andrea Phillips lost her father and nearly lost her son to the elements after an ill-fated backpacking trip to the mountains. Wyatt Merrill and his father Jack had risked their own lives to help, and she could never thank them enough. When her son Jeffrey struggles in the aftermath, she makes the move to Cherry Blossom Point to be closer to Wyatt and her new job writing an advice column for the local newspaper. She never expects to meet and lock horns with the town's grouchiest mechanic, and she certainly never expects to start wondering what that scruffy jawline would feel like beneath her fingertips...

Lena Merrill's wish has finally come true. Her family of two has just become a family of four, and she couldn't be happier. But even as baby Addy settles in quickly, young Sam is struggling. And who could blame him? He's suffered so much loss in his young life. Now it's up to Lena and Owen to prove that they are truly his forever family...and they aren't going anywhere.

Now that she's found a cache of buried treasure, PI Fallyn

Rappaport doesn't have to worry about money. She can take the cases that move her. When she hears about the kidnapping of six-year-old Wren "Birdie" Hazelton, she leaves Bluebird Bay and heads straight to Cherry Blossom Point to help. But when she arrives, she finds a tangled web of lies and deception.

Can she find Birdie before it's too late, or will this latest case end in tragedy?

ANDREA

Andrea set a stack of cardboard boxes down in her new home office and padded back into the living room, where Jack and Wyatt balanced her massive leather couch. They had turned it at an angle to get through the door and were working to hold it flat again.

"You want this in the center of the room or against the back wall?" Wyatt grunted, shooting her a quizzical glance.

"The back wall would be great. I seriously can't thank you guys enough!" Andrea reached up to pat Wyatt's shoulder on her way back to the moving van.

The past month had been the toughest of her life, and Wyatt and his dad had been the one, shining spot. Not only had they dropped everything to find her son Jeffrey and his grandpa when they were lost in the mountains, but they had gone out of their way to take Jeffrey under their wing and help Andrea ever since. She didn't know if they were partially motivated by guilt at not being able to get both of them out alive—not that they could've; her father had likely died almost instantly after his tragic fall—or if the heroic father and son would have gone this far for anyone in Cherry Blossom Point, but Andrea was thankful either way. In fact, she reminded herself sternly, she had a lot to be thankful for. Her new rental was perfect, a small three-bedroom place blocks from Jeffrey's new school. Better yet, it was only thirty minutes away from her mother, who had been mired in grief since the death of Andrea's dad.

But best of all?

Her son was alive and safe. There was a time not so long ago that she hadn't been sure that would be the case.

She sucked in a deep breath of cold, crisp air and blew it out in a puff of white. The first few days after the rescue, she'd been so elated her son was okay, she'd managed to block out the devastation of losing her father. But when the pain hit, it hit hard. She'd managed to hold it together and not break down, but there were still days that it was a struggle to get out of bed and go through the motions of life as if nothing had happened. As if her amazing, gentle, loving father hadn't been ripped away from her far too soon.

It was only when she'd caught him crying in the bathroom that she realized Jeffrey was struggling as much as she was. He hated going to school and didn't even care to play with friends anymore. In fact, being around Wyatt and participating in Jack's adventure school was the only thing that sparked joy for him these days. Initially, she'd been making the hour-long drive to Cherry Blossom Point for her son to participate and spend time with the Merrills and staying for the weekend, but that wasn't sustainable. Despite her initial concern about moving her son from one school to another in the middle of the semester, she was willing to move heaven and earth to see him smile. Picking up and moving was easy enough when she worked from home, and it would help her cement her new position as the Cherry Blossom Bee's advice columnist. So she'd used the short Thanksgiving break from school as their opportunity to make the move. Their old house was fresh on the market. The holidays weren't the best time to list, but if she didn't get a good offer soon, she could always find renters instead.

Given the fact that she'd seen Jeffrey laugh more today than she had in weeks, she was feeling good about her decision so far.

She snagged another box and paused as Jack dragged a heavy armchair from the van onto his back.

"Should you really be doing that alone?" Andrea asked. The man had just lost a finger to frostbite while rescuing her son, and he was still healing.

Behind her, Wyatt snorted a laugh. "Good luck trying to stop him," the teenager said.

"It was a finger. I have nine more," Jack deadpanned, his long strides eating up the frosty ground as he made his way to the front door again.

"End of discussion, I guess," she murmured, shooting Wyatt a helpless shrug.

She and Wyatt each carried a box into the house but were stopped at the door by a wide-eyed Jeffrey.

"Wyatt! Come see the basement! You aren't going to believe this. It has a dirt floor and all these hiding spots!"

Wyatt smiled fondly at him as he set his box on the floor in the foyer. "A root cellar?"

"Come see!" Jeffrey pulled on his arm, and Wyatt let the younger boy drag him away.

Andrea chuckled as she watched them go. Wyatt was

such a good kid, an amazing role model for her son. Neither of them had grown up with siblings, and they had formed a tight bond in the short time that they'd known each other. She supposed that surviving a snowstorm in the mountains of Maine could do that, but their connection seemed to go even deeper.

Kindred spirits.

Andrea set down the box she carried by the living room mantel and opened it. It was full of photos, and she couldn't resist setting some of them out right away. There was nothing like setting out family photos to make a house feel like home. Most of them showed Jeffrey at varying ages, starting with chubby baby cheeks and ending in a gap-toothed grin that had since filled in. A photo of Jeffrey and his grandpa put a lump in her throat.

He had been such an amazing dad to her, and a father figure for Jeffrey that was far better than the one nature had supplied. That deadbeat hadn't paid child support ever, and hadn't so much as seen his son since his first birthday. Good riddance. But Andrea's dad had been happy to fill in. Jeffrey was the son he'd never had, and Andrea's parents both adored him from the day he was born. Even before that, come to think of it. Andrea's mom had held her hand through doctor's appointments, and her dad had shown up to put Jeffrey's crib together when his real father couldn't be bothered. Ever since then, he had been the positive male role model for Jeffrey and an endless well of support to her.

Which meant that losing him had been a huge blow to both of them.

Andrea walked away from the pictures and grabbed a big box of kitchen stuff out of the moving van, which was nearly empty. When she carried the box though to the kitchen, she caught a glimpse of Jeffrey and Wyatt out the kitchen window. Jeffrey's face was animated as he gestured to the woods behind the house. Wyatt responded with almost the same level of enthusiasm. The two were probably making plans for survival shelters; Jeffrey was obsessed.

"This is the last of it," Jack said as he carried in two kitchen chairs and set them in place at Andrea's little table.

"Look at this," Andrea said. Jack joined her at the window and grinned at the sight of their boys gathering huge branches from the woods. "I'm so grateful for Wyatt. He's become like an older brother to Jeffrey."

"It's been good for Wyatt too," Jack acknowledged. "Sometimes we learn more as teachers than we do as students. It's given him a sense of direction and responsibility. He's grown up a lot this year."

"They do that. It's bittersweet."

"It sure as hell beats the alternative." A black hole seemed to open up in Jack's eyes, but a millisecond later, he blinked back to the present. "Jeffrey's a great kid. We love having him in our survival classes. Wyatt's thrilled to have you guys here in town."

The boys had disappeared from the backyard; a moment later they came tromping into the house.

"Hey Mom, do we still have that cider?"

"It's in the fridge."

Jeffrey poured two tall glasses of cider, and he and Wyatt gulped them down.

"Thank you so much for all of your help." Andrea pulled out a fifty-dollar bill she had tucked into her pocket and held it out to Wyatt. "I really appreciate it."

Wyatt waved her offering away. "So many people showed up for me when I was stuck in bed with a broken leg. I'm just paying it forward."

She knew from previous experience that he likely wouldn't take it, but she had to try. "Thanks, Wyatt. I'd been feeling pretty nervous about parenting through the teenage years, but you've allayed those fears for me."

"I don't know what allay means, but I'm going to guess from context that's a good thing?" Wyatt said, raising his brows comically.

"Mom's a writer." Jeffrey rolled his eyes. "She uses weird words a lot."

"Allay is not a weird word," she said, chuckling as she ruffled her son's hair. "And yes, to answer your question, Wyatt, it's a good thing.".

"Well, I wasn't always this easy," Wyatt admitted. "Pretty sure I gave my mom and dad more than one heart attack. But I think near death experiences have a mellowing effect. Like, hey, I'm still here! Better make the most of it, you know?"

Andrea smiled softly. It hit her in the chest, just like it did multiple times a day, an overwhelming implosion of mixed emotions. The grief of losing her father. The bone-deep gratitude that her son was still here.

"Would you join us for dinner tomorrow?" Jack asked. "The Merrill clan is gathering at my dad's place for Thanksgiving. There's always room for two more."

"That's very kind of you, but we'll be cooking our own Thanksgiving feast at my mom's house tomorrow." The first holiday without her dad was going to be rough on them all. "I really appreciate you asking, though."

"Absolutely. Family first." Jack said goodbye to each of

them with a firm handshake, which Jeffrey returned solemnly.

"Thanks again," Andrea murmured as she pulled Wyatt in for a hug.

"Anytime."

"And please," Jack added, "call or text if you need anything."

"Actually," Andrea said, "there is one thing. Can you recommend a good mechanic? My engine keeps squealing like there's a cat trapped under the hood."

"Absolutely. I'll text you the number and address of my guy."

"Thank you."

Jeffrey gave Wyatt's ribcage a quick squeeze and said, "I'm gonna go start clearing out a space for our shelter!"

"Good man!" Wyatt said. "Send me a photo."

"I will!"

Andrea's house emptied out, and she was left alone, staring at the towers of boxes waiting to be unpacked. But suddenly the house seemed foreign and far too quiet.

This was the first time she'd be living someplace her dad had never visited. No memories of joyous Christmas mornings. No ceiling fans he'd installed whirring overhead. No images of him pretending he wasn't napping on the recliner after a big Sunday meal.

She turned her back on the boxes and dug out a heating pad for her back. Then she opened up her laptop at the kitchen table. She had already chosen the next letter for her advice column, but she still needed to type up her response. Best to think about work right now instead of letting the ghosts in the corners of her mind drag her under.

Dear Andy -
My boyfriend has a habit of closing his laptop or exiting out of text messages on his phone whenever I walk by. He claims he isn't doing anything shady, but it makes me feel weird. I'd never snoop through his stuff, but part of me wants to. What do you think?
To Snoop or Not to Snoop.

She cracked her knuckles and dove in with a grim smile.
I'll be honest with you, Snoopy. If there's smoke, there's fire.

She fell into an almost trance-like rhythm as she clacked away at the keys. At some point, she was going to fall apart. The thin layer of glue holding her together would give, and she was going to have a full-on, messy, snot-crying breakdown.

But not today.

2

LENA

LENA HADN'T EXPECTED motherhood to be easy. She had been prepared for late nights, for tears and vomit and worried calls to the pediatrician. But she hadn't expected to be shut down before she'd even started.

Sam and Addy had been living with them for two weeks. Things with Addy had been so easy. Those baby snuggles were everything that Lena had dreamed of and longed for since Gemma's baby girl Cara had set off Lena's long-dormant biological clock.

But Addy's big brother, Sam? Lena felt like she hadn't made an inch of progress with him. He was a great kid. Kind and thoughtful. He wasn't overly fussy about what he ate or where they went. And the way he doted on his baby sister made it obvious that the kid had the capacity for deep love and connection.

Just not with her.

She understood it completely on an intellectual level. The poor little boy had lost both of his parents just a few months before. She hadn't expected him to bond with her immediately.

Or... maybe some deep, illogical, pie-in-the-sky piece of her had. Because two weeks of mothering a little boy who clearly didn't like her was weighing on her mind and heart. She wasn't looking for exuberant displays of love. She just wanted him to feel safe with her and Owen. To feel like she was getting through to him in some small way. And so far?

Zilch.

She felt like she was failing him.

"Are you okay, love?" Owen's strong hands kneaded Lena's shoulders in passing, pulling her out of the vortex of worry that had sucked her out of the present moment. She was supposed to be putting together the salad that was her meager contribution to the Merrill family's Thanksgiving feast. Instead, she had been staring unseeing into the salad bowl for nearly ten minutes.

"I'm fine." Lena flashed him a bright smile and went about putting the final touches on her big salad, but her lifelong best friend turned domestic partner wasn't so easily fooled. He wrapped his arms around her, and Lena dropped the knife she was holding and leaned into him.

"You're doing everything right," Owen murmured into her curls. "It's going to take time for him to learn that he can trust us. He's lost his parents, and he's barely been here long enough to catch his breath. Just give it time."

"You're right. I know you're right." Lena took a deep breath. "Should we bow out of the big family Thanksgiving and just put some pot pies in the oven instead?"

"Feeling that insecure about your salad, are you?"

Lena laughed weakly. "They've done well enough in

small doses, but the whole Merrill clan in one place at one time might be too much for the kids. Or for Sam, at least. Should I call my dad and explain? He'd understand."

"And deprive our children of Nikki's cooking?" Owen squeezed a ticklish spot just under Lena's ribcage, and she pushed away from him with a squeal. "Let's try, alright? If it's not going well, we leave. No big deal. Anyway, you wouldn't want this absurdly large and glorious salad to go to waste."

"True."

"So let's get this show on the road. I'll help the kids with their coats and boots."

"Okay. I'm almost ready."

Owen gave her one last squeeze and a kiss on the head before leaving the kitchen. "We knew it wasn't going to happen overnight, love. But it'll happen. We've got this."

"We've got this," Lena repeated on an exhale. A sudden wave of gratitude pushed her anxiety aside. She had Owen. They'd been entrusted with two beautiful children. There were a dozen people waiting in the wings, ready to help with anything they might need. Her business was chugging along despite Lena giving most of her time and attention to the kids.

She had everything she had ever wanted. Putting in the elbow grease to make it all work wasn't going to stop her.

"We've got this," she murmured under her breath like a prayer.

They were among the last to arrive at her dad's place and stepped straight into a full house. Sleepy Addy pressed her face into Lena's shoulder as she greeted her dad and siblings and nephew with one-armed hugs. Lena looked back to check on Sam and found him standing right next to the door, arms folded protectively across his chest.

Gayle took one look at the boy and pulled back on the hug, offering him a high-five instead. Lena watched some of Sam's anxiety fall away and even caught a hint of a smile as Gayle purposefully missed his hand and stumbled forward like she was about to fall.

When had her hard-ass older sister become so empathetic and thoughtful?

Kellan slipped an arm around Gayle's waist, asking Sam a quiet question that Lena didn't quite catch, and she grinned. Oh yeah. Right about when he came into the picture. Gayle had always been a good person with the best of intentions, but it had mostly manifested in over-the-top ways. It wasn't until her divorce that she had started to let go of her control freak tendencies that had been a bit of wedge between the siblings. And it wasn't until her relationship with Kellan that she had truly softened.

She liked this new Gayle.

A lot.

"Appetizers are ready," Nikki announced.

"Only your family does proper appetizers on Thanksgiving," Owen murmured in Lena's ear.

She grinned up at him. "And?"

"And it's ridiculous. And I love it. Are those bite-size pecan pies? Nikki, have I told you lately that I love you?"

Lena smiled and shook her head as Owen gave her kid sister a kiss on the cheek and then stuffed an entire not-quite-bite-size pecan tart in his mouth.

"Sam, you have to try these."

"Beth's here!" Nikki sprinted out the front door to greet her daughter. It was a full five minutes before Beth made it past the other Merrills and Lena was able to pull her into a hug. Lena's niece had her mother's dark curls and a lovely smile that reminded Lena so much of her own mother. She loved her with her whole heart.

"There's my new baby cousin," Beth cooed, making Addy smile. "I made you something." She reached into her purse and pulled out a little hat knitted in a pinwheel pattern out of varicolored yarn. She pulled it onto Addy's head and smiled. "Perfect fit."

"Beth, I love it. Thank you!" Lena hugged her again, blinking back tears.

"We've got some milestones to catch up on." Beth's gaze landed on Sam, who was half hidden behind Owen. "Hey, Sammy!" she said, popping a squat to get on eye level with the little boy. "I'm your big cousin, Beth. I don't know if you know this, but I'm kind of obsessed with knitting things. In this family, everybody gets a hat." She pulled one out of her bag and held it out to him. Sam hesitated, and then slowly reached for it, turning it over in his hands with an uncertain expression. "Try it on, would you? If it's the wrong size, I'll fix it by Christmas."

Sam tried the cap on—another perfect fit. His was blue with a single, emerald pine tree.

"Looks great," Beth said, winning a shy smile from Sam.

How easy Beth made it look...

Lena swallowed hard and headed into the kitchen to warm up a bottle for Addy. When she came back into the living room, her niece was entertaining Sam with cheesy magic tricks, which he seemed to be wholeheartedly enjoying. Lena felt a bittersweet twinge at the huge grin on his face. She only ever saw him smile like that when Addy did something new. But Beth was pretty darn lovable. Wyatt joined in, and soon half of the family was competing for Sam's attention, which he seemed happy enough to give.

Addy had just fallen asleep after half a bottle when there was a knock on the door.

"Who are we missing?" Lena asked, looking around the room. Everyone they were expecting for dinner was already here. Jack opened the door, and a general cry of *"Anna!"* went up around the room.

"Surprise!" Anna called.

Jack greeted their half-sister with a warm hug—quite the one-eighty from telling her that she wasn't welcome in Cherry Blossom Point, much less in their family home more than a year before.

"What a wonderful surprise!" Eric embraced her, clearly elated to have all of his children in one place.

It warmed her to the core, thinking how far their family had come in such a short time. They had all grown so much, and she felt like it had all started with Nikki bringing Anna into the fold.

"Where's Beckett?" Lena asked when Anna finally made it over to her.

"He's with his son and their family." Anna smiled down at Addy's sleeping face. "We're all meeting up for a late dinner at Steph's. The family just keeps getting bigger and bigger. It's hard to keep up!"

"Tell me about it." Lena laughed and squeezed Anna's hand. Most of her life, she hadn't even known that Anna existed. It had been a deep, dark secret that their parents had hidden for decades. Now Anna was just another one of her sisters, and Lena loved her as dearly as the three siblings she had grown up with.

That love was a powerful reminder that lives could collide in strange and tragic ways and still create beautiful family connections.

Anna drifted off to talk to Beth, and Lena settled deeper into her dad's comfiest chair. Addy was sound asleep, a warm weight on her chest, and Lena relished the feeling. There was something so perfectly fulfilling about just holding a sleeping baby. Just being there for her, being her safe space. And as she watched Sam laughing with Beth and Wyatt, new hope bubbled up in her chest. There was a place for Sam here, in this family, and Lena was just one part of the beautiful whole. He was going to be okay. Better than okay. And, in time, their bond would grow, just as the one between her and Anna had.

Addy was awake and animated again by the time they all finally settled in around the dinner table, which was at capacity even at full extension with all of its leaves. Lena was touched to see that her family had dug an old high chair out of the garage and set it at the table for Addy.

"No Gemma today?" Anna observed, glancing around.

"She and Patrick decided to keep it simple their first Thanksgiving together," Owen told her. "Just them and the kids." He chuckled as a general "*aww*" went up around the table. "Yes, it's all very sweet. And Patrick is almost good enough for her, so I'll let it slide that he's hogging my baby sister and my nephews on Thanksgiving."

Lena squeezed Owen's knee under the table, smiling at his halfhearted blustering. She knew how grateful he was that

15

his sister had found happiness again after the gutting loss of her husband and the father of her children the year before. It was the fresh start that they all deserved.

Lena's eyes drifted down the table to Sam, who appeared to be content, squeezed in between Wyatt and Beth, and she made a mental note to talk to Gemma. Her pseudo-sister-in-law had been busy these past few weeks, but maybe she would have some insight as to how to help Sam process his grief and all the changes in his life.

"Potatoes?"

She accepted a heavy bowl from Jack with a smile of thanks.

One thing she wasn't about to do was waste this day on thinking of the bad things in life. She shoved her worries to the back of her mind and focused on enjoying Nikki's spectacular Thanksgiving feast. Time passed in a pleasant blur of conversation and food, punctuated by her random attempts to keep Addy's bowl of creamed yams on the plate as opposed to on the floor.

"I need a break before pie," Beth announced as the meal wound down. "Auntie Lena, can Sam play Mario Kart with Wyatt and me? It's really fun, and there's no violence in it or anything."

Sam shot her a hopeful glance, and she nodded. "Sure."

"Thanks!" Sam said, rushing off from the table. Lena's heart gave a funny little lurch in her chest as she watched him go. She turned her attention back to Addy, who wore more yams than clothing at this point.

"Let's get you cleaned up, little miss." She lifted the sticky baby out of the high chair and carried her into the kitchen, where Corinne and Anna were already finishing off the first round of dishes. As Anna started the dishwasher going, Corinne glanced at her phone and sighed.

"What's wrong?" Anna asked. She took one look at Addy and handed Lena a roll of paper towels.

"Sorry." Corinne flashed them an apologetic smile, and her expression dimmed again. "I was just checking the local news. I can't stop thinking about that little girl who went missing yesterday."

"The Hazelton girl?" Lena's heart sank. Six-year-old Wren Hazelton had disappeared in the middle of the night. Initially, Lena had hoped the girl had walked to her neighbor's house before dawn or something, that there was just some confusion that might be cleared up a few hours later. But as the time stretched on, the local anchors were starting to use the dreaded word...

Kidnapped.

"They haven't found her yet?"

Corinne shook her head. "Her poor parents."

"She goes to the same school as Aiden and Zoe," Lena murmured.

"There are no leads at all, according to the news."

Lena slipped a clean, dry dress over Addy's head and pulled her baby girl in close for a hug. She had seen enough crime dramas to know that these early hours were the most crucial... but they had gone the whole day without news. The girl's father was a wealthy and powerful man, US representative Graham Hazelton, and at this point, the town's hopes were pinned on the idea that it might be a ransom situation. But so far... nothing. No note, no call. Just... poof. Into thin air.

"That's horrifying," Anna said quietly. "It's always such a shock when something like that happens in a small town."

"So scary," Lena murmured.

"I remember when a girl disappeared in Bluebird Bay like it was yesterday..." Anna trailed off and sighed. "It was more than two decades before her mother got any closure. I hope they find her soon."

"Just not knowing where my daughter was for like an hour last year was torture," Corinne said. "I can't imagine having your baby girl disappear from her bed, no leads, no nothing."

Addy squirmed, and Lena loosened her grip, realizing that she had been hugging her just a bit too tight.

"We're ready for pie," Gayle called as she popped her head into the kitchen.

"Then pie you shall have," Nikki announced, pushing past her. "Give me ten minutes to warm up the apple-blueberry and whip up some cream for the pumpkin."

"I can do the whipped cream," Gayle offered.

Lena exchanged a sad smile with Anna and Corinne, letting her own happy family push the worrying local news story out of the spotlight. Her heart lifted as Sam came into the kitchen looking for Beth.

"She's just helping get the pie ready," she said, instinctively leaning in to give him an affectionate squeeze on the shoulder.

Sam jerked away like she'd pinched him, and Lena tried not to let the hurt show on her face.

She was a naturally affectionate person, but she needed to take a page out of Gayle's book here. From now on, she would do her best to take a beat and read his body language before she touched him.

"Can I hold her?" Anna asked, reaching for Addy, who was more than happy to change hands.

Lena handed over her little bundle of joy and made a beeline for the sink, rolling up the sleeves of her sweater as she went.

Time. That was the key.

She just needed to be patient, and in time, she and Sam would form their own bond...

Wouldn't they?

3

ANDREA

"Mom, you're driving like ten miles an hour below the speed limit."

"Am I?" Andrea covered her nervous laugh with a cough. She tried to stay steady for her son, but these days it seemed her nervous system was stretched to the limit.

Thanksgiving without her dad had been brutal. Her mom was wrecked and had completely and uncharacteristically botched her half of their meal for three. The turkey was dry, and the casseroles had baked to something resembling charcoal. Andrea's lackluster sides hadn't exactly made up the difference, but Jeffrey had still put a decent dent in the mashed potatoes and gravy. There had been enough to eat, and the pumpkin pie had almost made up for the lack of turkey and cranberry sauce. Still, they had decided as a family that they would be getting Chinese food for Christmas. Maybe next year they would be able to pull off their old family traditions. This year, Andrea was done fighting for some semblance of a normal family holiday.

She was tapped out.

The loss of her dad was still hitting her in bits and pieces, as if she were making her way barefoot across a glass-strewn floor. She paused to pick out what pieces she could while other shards worked their way deeper, always too preoccupied with getting her son across unscathed to really take the time to heal. She had mostly managed that, at least—getting Jeffrey through it. Keeping him in close contact with Wyatt had been his salvation. And she had taken care of her mother as best as she could. Eventually, she needed to pause and take care of herself.

At least they were officially moved into their new place, though. More than half of their boxes were unpacked, and she had easy access to all of the stuff they needed day to day. Her back was sore from the work, but her heart was relieved. Maybe now, with the move behind them and Jeff spending the weekend with Wyatt, Jack, and a small group of other kids working on survival skills, she would finally have the chance to process everything that had happened.

"You guys are going to have such a great time," Andrea said as she pulled into the parking lot of Jack's school. "I'm actually jealous."

"Oh...well, maybe you could come one time," he said dubiously before rushing to add, "But like, not today, though, okay?" He shot her a worried look and instantly tried to backtrack, bless his sensitive little heart. "Unless you really want to, I mean."

She chuckled and pulled him into a hug. "No way. This is your special thing. I'm just excited for you to come show me what you learned when you get home on Sunday. You can tell me all about it over pizza for dinner, how does that sound?" Andrea asked. He shot her a smile and nodded.

"Deal."

He jumped out of the car and scurried toward the school, letting out a whoop of excitement when Wyatt met him at the door. Andrea let out an explosive breath as she watched him go. The next couple days would be the longest time he'd spent away from her since the ill-fated hike with her dad. She wasn't sure she was ready for it yet, but Jeffrey clearly was, and that was what mattered. She refused to allow herself to become a helicopter parent, but dang... Motherhood was a kick in the teeth sometimes.

As she pulled away from the school, a Missing poster caught her eye. Below a picture of a sweet-faced girl were three-inch letters that read *Wren Hazelton*. She went to Jeffrey's new school. The story had been all over the news. Mostly, the press featured her father, Graham, begging for the return of his daughter. A shell-shocked woman with golden hair had stood a few feet behind him—Alicia, the mother.

Andrea's heart lurched as she drove past the photo. She knew what it felt like to have a kid missing, albeit not under these same circumstances. Every hour felt like a day, every day like a week.

Should she send something to the mother, maybe? Andrea wondered as she drove across town. A homemade meal, a note of encouragement with a prayer for her daughter's safety? Andrea wanted to reach out somehow, but she also didn't want to intrude on the woman's privacy. Maybe Jack would know if anyone in town had set up a meal train or something of the sort. She made a mental note to ask him as she followed her GPS to Spivey's Auto, the name of the garage he'd recommended.

As she parked in the small lot outside of the garage, the omnipresent anxiety that she had felt since the loss of her dad ratcheted up a few notches. A shady mechanic had obscenely overcharged her once when she was a young mother. It was a month's worth of income she'd barely been able to scrape together. Her dad had been furious, and he'd handled all of her car maintenance himself after that.

But he wasn't here anymore.

Andrea swallowed and took a deep breath, refusing to look at the black hole of grief that opened up in her chest whenever she dwelled too long on the loss of her dad. It was time to learn how to handle this herself.

"Be confident," she murmured as she tucked her keys into the outer pocket of her purse. "Be firm. Don't take any crap."

There was no one in the lackluster waiting room when she walked in. Pausing at the door, she stood in silence to see if the bell that had jingled upon her arrival had summoned anyone from the back, but no one came.

"Hello?" she called.

"Yeah?" a low, male voice replied before a figure stepped into the reception area. For a moment, Andrea was stunned into silence.

At well over six feet of leanly-packed muscle, he was a lot of man. So much so that he gave unexpected shape to the blue coveralls that would've hung like a gunny sack on most anyone else. When she finally managed to look him in the face, she found that he wasn't movie star attractive. His strong nose was slightly crooked, like it had been broken once or twice before, and the dark five o'clock shadow just added to the tough-guy vibe he gave off.

She wouldn't have said a man like that was her type, but

as she opened her mouth to speak, no words came out. That had literally never happened before. It wasn't like her to go all empty-headed at the sight of an attractive guy. Clearly, it was yet another symptom of all the recent upheaval in her life.

Maybe she needed... a breathwork course or something. Maybe therapy.

Probably therapy.

"Can I help you?" His voice was so deep now that it was more like a growl. His dark eyes pierced through her, and it was another moment before she could pull a sentence together.

"Yes, um...yes, I made an appointment the other day?" She had spoken to a woman on the phone who said that they would squeeze her in. "My car's been making a loud noise. I'm not sure why."

He grunted and hunched over the date book on the counter. "Receptionist is on a coffee run, and her shorthand is atrocious. But I'll take a look. Might not get to it until this afternoon. In the middle of something right now." He held a hand out, and Andrea just looked at it. "Keys?" he asked, wiggling his fingers impatiently.

"Oh. Um..." Andrea hesitated, one hand in the pocket of her purse. "The lady I spoke to said you have loaners available?"

"One's already out," he said gruffly, "and I've been using the other one, but I walked to work today. I can run and grab it after I finish this job, and you can pick it up around noon if you really need some wheels."

She blinked at him as she digested his words. Without a car, her whole morning would basically be shot. She had really been counting on getting some stuff for the new house. Wrinkling her nose, she glanced through the dirty front window at the cars in the lot. There was a Mustang that she figured belonged to the mechanic, but there was also a serviceable-looking little Honda parked there.

"What about those?"

He sighed as he moved towards the door to the garage. "Mine and my receptionist's."

Andrea pointed toward an old, black Chevy in the far corner of the lot. "What about the truck?"

"Nope."

She looked back at him, surprised by the ice in his clipped response.

It was only then that she noticed the name sewn onto the pocket of his coveralls.

Cole.

Like what he deserved to get in his stocking, only spelled wrong, she thought spitefully.

"Why not the truck? I can drive a stick, if that's the issue..."

"Not an option, end of story," he growled. "Keys?"

She handed him her keys hesitantly. What a jerk. She would've made arrangements if the receptionist hadn't mentioned the loaner...

"Well, what am I supposed to do between now and noon?" she asked, frowning.

He made a sharp gesture toward the door. "Take a walk into town? It's not far."

"It's freezing outside!"

He was already halfway through the garage door as he called back over his shoulder,

"Walk fast."

Andrea stared after him for a moment, bewildered. When the whir of shop tools made it apparent that he wouldn't be coming back to apologize, she pulled out her phone and looked at a map to get her bearings. Less than half a mile to Sadie's café. That was manageable, she supposed. Although she was half-tempted to take her car, drive off, and find another mechanic. But Jack had told her that this was the guy he used. And he must be good at what he did to keep a business running with such piss-poor customer service.

She deliberated for another minute before she finally tossed her keys on the counter and headed for the door.

What kind of name was Cole, anyway? Probably his birth certificate read Mervin or something equally mundane, and he'd dubbed himself Cole to sound cool.

Andrea tucked her head close to her chest against the cold and stepped into the blustery wind with a hiss. She might have waved the white flag this time, but just let him even try to overcharge her for his services. He'd find out very quickly that she wasn't as nice as she looked. If she had to, she'd go toe to toe with that mountain of a man in honor of her dad. And given that she was a woman precariously close to the edge? She had her money on herself.

Her shivering lips split into a grim smile.

Mr. Cole Spivey didn't know who he was messing with.

4

BOBBIE

Bobbie eyeballed the fixings-to-turkey ratio and plopped one more scoop of sausage and sage stuffing onto the thick-cut slab of multi-grain bread she'd bought from the bakery that morning.

She liked Thanksgiving food.

But she looooved day after, leftover sandwiches even more.

She topped her creation with a dollop of cranberry sauce before capping it off with another piece of bread and then paused thoughtfully. Would Gemma like hers with or without the controversial condiment?

She swiped her hands on a nearby dish towel and tapped out a quick text on her cell phone.

Cranberry sauce or no?

Three dots rolled across the screen a moment before her friend's reply popped up.

DEAR GOD NO. Mayo please :)

Bobbie grinned, shaking her head as she headed back to the fridge for the requested mayonnaise.

She was really looking forward to her lunch date with Gemma today. Between Patrick and his daughter Zoe moving in with Gemma and the boys and Bobbie's newly redefined relationship with Marcus, they hadn't seen much of each other these past few weeks. Sure, they talked and texted daily, but she was craving some face-to-face time with her friend.

Not that she'd have changed things even if she could have. Nope, things had turned out better than she could've ever dreamed. Despite hiding her son Archie from his father for months before coming clean, Marcus had found it in his heart to not only forgive her, but to love her.

She couldn't believe her luck and vowed never to take it— or him—for granted.

And now they were together. Still best friends just like before, but so much more. Co-parenting Archie and getting to share all the little milestones in his life with Marcus was heaven.

As if summoned by the thought, her phone chimed with a text image. She swiped on the message, and her heart melted as she stared down at her baby boy perched on his daddy's hip. The pair of them were pink-cheeked and beaming as they both pointed to a massive spruce tree.

What do you think? We're going to name him Big Blue!

She chuckled to herself as she shot back her reply.

Perfect!

It so wasn't. She'd imagined a Christmas tree half that size. That behemoth would take up the vast majority of her living room, but she didn't care. Those smiles were worth being a little cramped for the next month or so.

K, we still got to dig him out and then we're stopping off for hot chocolate.

She shot back a red heart emoji and then set down her phone to finish prepping lunch. By the time she'd finished making the sandwiches along with a Caesar salad to work some greens into the meal, Gemma was calling through the now-open front door.

"Knock knock, it's me!"

"In the kitchen!" Bobbie hollered back as she poured them each a champagne flute of sparkling water.

"Oooh, fancy," Gemma cooed when she walked in, waggling her brows. "Given the fact that my breakfast consisted of four pieces of leftover pineapple I scooped off Cara's highchair tray and the crust from Aiden's toast, I'm loving how extra this is."

"Nothing but the best for you, Gem. Here, give me your coat."

Gemma shrugged out of her forest green parka and gave a little shiver. "Remind me to float the idea of a dual family vacation to someplace warm next winter. Key West, or the Bahamas or something. I think I'm getting soft in my old age."

"Old, my eye." Bobbie let out a snort. "How do you think I feel coming from down south? It's not even December yet, and I'm already rocking long johns."

She slung her friend's coat over the back of a chair, and they both took their seats.

"This looks awesome," Gemma said, pausing to take a sip of her sparkling water. "And the fact that I get to eat sitting down, and talking to another adult without a dozen interruptions is just icing on the cake. I feel like I'm getting away with something."

Bobbie grinned as she watched Gemma tuck into her holiday sandwich with gleeful abandon. "What is Patrick doing with the kids today?"

Gemma held up a finger and finished the massive bite she'd taken before replying. "He took them all to pick out a Christmas tree. I told him I'd go with him, but he insisted I take a few hours for myself."

"Shut up! That's what Marcus and Archie are doing too. Camden's Farm?"

"Yup."

"Marcus chose the biggest one on the lot, I'm pretty sure, so at least you'll be spared that." Bobbie took a bite of her own sandwich and let out a groan. It was the perfect balance of sweet and salty, and the softness of the stuffing against the crusty loaf made it a textural delight.

"So good, right?" Gemma said with a nod. "You can make me lunch any day."

"I'm hoping now that you guys are settled in and Marcus and I have found a routine that works, we'll get back to doing this kind of thing more. How was your first holiday all together?"

Gemma cocked her head, looking thoughtful. "Like... joyful chaos, I guess?" She barked out a laugh and shrugged. "Aiden and Zoe are still in the honeymoon stage of besties living in the same house, so it's a battle to get them to treat it like the norm instead of a slumber party. Just seeing her smile again has been so good, though, it's hard to deny her anything. She isn't quite herself yet, but she's definitely improving. Being out of that house has helped."

Zoe's mother had abandoned the little girl for the second time, leaving Cherry Blossom Point—and her daughter—

behind. Gemma and Patrick had opted to finally move on the feelings they had for each other and blend their families together in Gemma's home as the constant reminders of Zoe's mom in their house were causing her pain. It was a move that was clearly working for them. Her friend looked the best she'd ever seen her. Like she was wearing her happiness all over her face. A far cry from the perpetually exhausted and grieving woman she'd met at their Mommy and Me classes last spring.

"How about you? How was your Thanksgiving?" Gemma asked, forking up a bite of salad.

She'd gotten to celebrate the holiday early with her siblings and mom when she'd gone down to check on Marcus's dad in the hospital a few weeks before, so she was off the hook with the family. It had just been her, Marcus, and the baby.

"It was really lovely. We ate our faces off and then played board games after Archie went to sleep."

She still felt like pinching herself sometimes. The fact that he'd forgiven her despite missing their son's birth and so much more? It was like a miracle. A wave of guilt rolled over her, and she consciously shoved it aside. Marcus may have forgiven her, but she still needed to figure out how to fully forgive herself.

It was a work in progress.

"Oh!" Gemma gasped, setting down her fork and leaning in. "Did you hear about the little girl from Aiden's school who was kidnapped?"

Bobbie gnawed on the inside of her cheek, instantly anxious at the thought. "Wren Hazelton. It's awful. I'm actually hoping to run a special edition of the Bee. Just a two page leaflet asking people who might have any information to come forward. Marcus offered to fund a ten thousand dollar reward for any leads that pan out. We just have to wait for the approval from the family before we print and put them out."

The missing girl would've been on her mind a lot even before Archie, but now that she was a mother herself, it felt that much more personal. She and Marcus had stayed up late the night before talking through their own fears as parents and brainstorming ways to help. She shrugged and shook her head slowly.

"I know it's probably a long shot, but it's something."

"I think that's a great idea, and surely getting the word out to as many people as possible is a good thing." Gemma looked away, wincing. "I can't even imagine what her parents are going through. I just pray that she's found safe. Aiden and Zoe have been asking all sorts of questions. I don't want to lie to them, but at the same time, I don't want them living in fear. This town is about as safe as a place can get... or at least it always has been." She blew out a breath. "I'm just going to hope for a positive outcome. I can't help but think that, due to her father's position, this might all be a ransom situation or something."

"It's definitely a possibility," Bobbie agreed. "In which case it's in the kidnapper's best interest to keep her alive and well."

The pair of them ate in silence for a few minutes before Bobbie changed the subject to something less distressing. By the time they got to dessert—leftover sweet potato pie with fresh whipped cream—the melancholy had lifted some, and Gemma had Bobbie whooping with laughter at a story about Aiden when he was little coloring on the walls with crayon.

"So he actually signed Liam's name underneath his drawing?"

"Not only did he sign it, he put 'I am Liam and I wrote this.'" Gemma wiped a tear of mirth from her eye. "And when I asked Aiden if he did it, he shrugs, points at the wall, and goes, 'Mama, it says wight hewe. Wiam wote it,' and then he walks away. Case dismissed."

"Hilarious. He's a diabolical genius. How did you keep a straight face?"

"I had to go to my bedroom for a few minutes until I could keep it together. Then we had to have a talk about honesty and blaming others for our actions. I did take a picture of it, though, just to show them when they get older," Gemma said with a grin.

They were just finishing their dessert when the front door swung open.

"We're here!" Marcus called. "And guess who we ran into!"

There was no need for guessing as Zoe and Aiden came barreling into the kitchen, white Styrofoam cups in hand. "Do you have any cookies?" Aiden asked, shooting a hopeful glance at Bobbie.

"Chocolate chip would be ideal, but we'll take anything," Zoe piped in before stopping short with a scowl. "Except oatmeal raisin. Raisins are a pox on mankind."

"A pox, huh?" Bobbie said, her lips twitching as she tried not to burst out laughing. "Let me see what I can scare up that might fit the bill."

"We brought you guys hot chocolates from Sadie's," Liam

said, two cups extended as he entered the kitchen with Patrick trailing behind him.

"Oooh, thank you," Gemma said, taking the cups from him and setting them on the table. She let out a bark of laughter as Patrick came into full view, Archie on his hip, Cara snuggled against his chest in a sling. "You've got a lot of babies there! Want me to take one off your hands?"

Patrick grinned. "No way. These cuties are my excuse not to have to help Marcus lug that Christmas tree into the house."

A loud thump followed by a muffled groan rang out from the living room.

"I'm okay," Marcus called, clearly out of breath. "Almost got this bad boy through the door."

Patrick blew out a sigh and handed Archie off to Gemma.

"My conscience can't take it," he muttered as he extricated Cara from the sling.

Bobbie set a package of Oreos on the table for the kids and reached for the baby. "I've got her."

"Come on, Liam. Let's show Marcus how to get a twelve-foot tree through a six-foot door, shall we?"

Liam popped off a salute, and the two headed out of the kitchen to rescue their friend.

As Bobbie looked around the kitchen, she couldn't help but grin. Aiden and Zoe were happily deconstructing their sandwich cookies, then dipping them into their cocoa before popping them into their chocolate-ringed mouths. Cara was tugging at Bobbie's mistletoe earring as Archie blew raspberries at Gemma. In the distance, she could hear Liam, Patrick, and Marcus strategizing.

"On the count of three...ready?"

Gemma was spot on. It was joyful chaos, and she wouldn't trade it for the world. In that moment, everything seemed perfect...

And then she thought of Wren Hazelton, and her stomach sank.

She wasn't the first child to go missing. She wouldn't be the last. But Wren was a part of this little coastal town that had become home for Bobbie, and she mattered.

Please, God, let this sweet child come home safe for the holidays.

Please.

5

ANDREA

A BRISK WALK and a healthy dose of righteous indignation kept Andrea from freezing on her way to Sadie's café. She hadn't been dressed for a stroll in the icy November winds, and the warm air inside the little restaurant was slow to relieve the chill that had seeped into her bones.

She was still irritated as she waited in the long line, but a wide, welcoming smile from Sadie when she reached the counter calmed her nerves enough that she was able to give Wyatt's mom a genuine smile in return.

"So glad you stopped in! How have you guys been? Starting to get settled into your new place?"

"Yeah, we're mostly unpacked, and Jeff starts school on Monday."

"That's great! I hope he likes it. Cherry Blossom Point is a really wonderful place for kids. I think he'll make friends quickly."

"I hope so. In the meantime, his surrogate big brother is keeping his spirits up. You raised a good one there."

"I love that," Sadie said warmly. "Filling that role has

been so good for Wyatt, too. It's really steadied him and given him a sense of purpose. He seems like he's grown up so much."

"Well, we're truly grateful for him every day." Andrea glanced over her shoulder at the growing line and gave the old man behind her an apologetic smile. "Sorry, I'll order so you can get back to work. I'll have a double shot latte and your cheddar-bacon breakfast sandwich."

"You've got it." Sadie reached out for her credit card, but Andrea hesitated.

"If I order to go, do you offer delivery or—?"

"We do."

"I'm thinking of sending Alicia Hazelton some food. Seeing her on the news just about tears my heart out every time. Maybe that and a note... sympathy and hope and all that, from someone who just went through something similar? I don't know, maybe it's not a good idea..."

"I think it's a lovely idea," Sadie said with an encouraging smile.

Andrea perused the baked goods, focused on finding something that a person could get down even when fear made it hard to stomach anything at all. "How about a box of the lemon-ginger muffins? And a few of those orange-cranberry scones?"

"Done. Do you need some paper for the note?"

"That would be great, Sadie. Thank you."

"My pleasure. I'll throw in some macaroons on the house and a note of my own as well."

"You're the best." With parents like Sadie and Jack, it was easy to see where Wyatt got his kind nature.

Andrea paid for her order and snagged the last free table.

Sadie came by a few minutes later with a piece of nice stationery paper.

"Do you need a pen?"

"I always have a pen, but thanks for saving me from writing a sympathetic note on a scrap of notebook paper."

"Anytime. Your breakfast should be out in just a minute. I'm overdue for a break, if you'd like some company."

"I'd love that."

Sadie disappeared into the back, and Andrea pulled her best pen out of her purse. What could she possibly write to a stranger that might bring her some shred of comfort?

There was nothing, so she settled on simple and to the point.

Eat something and keep your strength up if you can, she scrawled at last. *We're praying for you.*

She signed the note and handed it to Sadie when the other women set their food and drinks on the table.

Sadie pocketed the stationery and said, "Great. Our delivery girl should be back soon, and I'll send her right back out with this."

"Thanks." Andrea took a bite of her croissant sandwich, and a little bit of the tension gripping her melted away. The herb-infused eggs were cooked perfectly, topped with melted cheese and crispy bacon. "This is phenomenal."

"It's a customer favorite," Sadie said with a grin. She took a bite of her own meal, a massive, loaded salad that Andrea would have been tempted to order for later if she wouldn't have had to schlep it back to the garage where she had left her car.

"So Jeffrey was telling me that he and Wyatt are talking about taking a little ski trip."

"Yeah! Is that okay?" Sadie asked, raising a brow. "It's not a big resort or anything, just a little family-run lodge that we've been going to for years. Wyatt said that you wanted to ease Jeffrey back into mountain adventures."

Andrea nodded slowly. "He loves it so much. Forest adventures have always been such a big part of his life, from walks in the woods as a baby to forest preschool to camping trips with his grandpa. I didn't want to let what happened ruin it for him or make him afraid. And so far, so good, thanks to Wyatt. Jeffrey is doing really well, all things considered. My own fear is a little tougher to cope with."

"I hear that."

"But it's good. He's so excited. He adores Wyatt. And this is exactly what he needs."

"You're a wonderful mom, Andrea."

She blinked back tears, surprised by just how much she needed to hear those words right now. When a person came *this* close to losing their child, guilt could really wreak havoc on a body.

"Thank you. Takes one to know one."

Sadie smiled and drained the last of her coffee. "We're a little short staffed today, so I've got to get back to it. Thanks for letting me join you."

"I'm glad you did."

"See you soon. I'll remind Wyatt to send you all the details on that trip."

"Thanks."

Andrea took a deep breath of the brisk air as she stepped outside, tummy full and ready for the chilly walk back to the auto shop. The delicious breakfast and hot coffee had bolstered her almost as much as her conversation with Sadie.

She had made the right decision when she moved here, for her and Jeffrey both. And that was one huge weight off of her mind.

By the time she stepped through the front door of the auto shop, though, her shoulders were hunched tight, and she was shivering again.

She found Cole sitting at the reception desk. His hands were clean, and he was eating a sandwich out of a wax-paper bag. He looked her straight in the eye when she walked in but didn't stand or say a word of greeting. She cleared her throat and spoke up, determined not to let the man's deep brown eyes and brusque personality catch her off guard again.

"Did you have a chance to look at my car?"

He nodded and swallowed the bite he'd been working on. "Problem with the timing belt."

Andrea's stomach sank. That sounded expensive. She straightened, lifting her chin. "Does it need to be replaced?"

"No. Belt's fine."

"So..." Andrea prompted, tilting her head to one side.

"One of the pulley units is screwed up."

"Let me guess," she said with a sigh. "That's even more expensive?"

"Nah. Some places would replace the whole thing, but I can just swap out that one piece."

Interesting.

So maybe Cole wasn't *all* bad.

"And did everything look okay besides that?" she pressed.

The mechanic gave a single, curt nod. "Yep. Car's in great shape. You've done a good job maintaining it."

A sudden pain sliced Andrea's chest, and her throat tightened as she fought back tears. There it was again, that sharp stab of grief that nearly took her out at the knees. No way was she about to let this guy see her cry, though.

She cleared her throat and said briskly, "Yes, well, my dad took care of maintenance for me."

Another nod and a grunt. "It's going to take a day or so for me to get the part you need, and I don't recommend driving it between now and then. Could cause more damage." The door opened behind Andrea with a jingle, and the mechanic added, "This is Starla. She can take care of the rest."

A woman closer to twenty than thirty flipped her jet black hair over one shoulder and directed a dazzling grin across the counter.

"I'm headed to the garage," Cole said. "Just give this lady the keys to the Subaru."

"Andrea," she interjected with a quick smile. "My name is Andrea."

He stared at her blankly and shrugged. "Okay. Give *Andrea* the keys to the Subaru."

Alrighty, then.

"Will do," Starla called at his retreating back. Andrea was oddly relieved to see the man being as rude to his receptionist as he had been to her. Which meant she wasn't especially annoying or anything; Cole Spivey was just a cranky son of a gun.

A moment later, his broad shoulders and dark hair disappeared through the swinging door.

Starla cleared her throat, and when Andrea turned to face her, the younger woman gave her a long look as she snapped and popped her chewing gum.

She was beautiful in an edgy sort of way, with heavy eyeliner and a silver ring through one arched eyebrow.

"So a loaner car then?" Starla cracked her gum.

"Yes please."

Starla pulled some papers out of a drawer and slapped them down on the counter. "Sign there."

Andrea scanned the agreement before filling in her name and signing the bottom, and Starla handed her the keys. Andrea checked her watch on the way out, forcing herself to slow down and take a breath. Still plenty of time to get loads done today. No harm, no foul.

As she walked through the parking lot, her gaze caught on Cole's heavy boots sticking out from under a car. Steel-toed, she supposed, so that all of the people he irritated into stomping on his feet didn't crush his toes. Andrea clutched the key she held and looked away.

She had gotten what she wanted, so why did she still feel so annoyed? What advice would she give if this very scenario was sent in to Ask Andy?

Dear Under My Skin,

Either accept that your mechanic has crummy people skills or take your business elsewhere in the future. His job is to fix your car, not stroke your ego. If you can't adjust your expectations, find another mechanic who meets them— because you're not going to change this one.

Andrea kicked a stray pebble out of her path and unlocked the Subaru, forcing herself to take some calming breaths.

What did she care about her mechanic's attitude? She just needed a car that wouldn't catch fire halfway between here and her mom's house. The guy's bad mood wasn't her problem.

So why couldn't she get his scowling face out of her head?

6

FALLYN

FALLYN RAPPAPORT RELEASED the tension in her shoulders, doing her best to take things one moment at a time as Shaw pulled into the rocky driveway of the cozy-looking bed and breakfast. The yard was pristine, despite the now-bare trees. It was sure to be a far cry from the amazing bed and breakfast in Bluebird Bay that had resulted in Fallyn finding both a mother-figure and best friend in her host, Molly, but it was good to see that the exterior of this place at least lived up to the pictures from the listing.

Her life had changed so much in the past year. She'd left her job as an investigative journalist, become a private investigator, and fallen in love with her business partner. The craziest part of it all? Her quest to find a pirate's treasure off the coast of Maine had come to a victorious end. She and her four cohorts had wound up unearthing tens of millions of dollars' worth of coins, relics, and jewelry. The resulting wealth had been a blessing for each and every one of them.

Molly had decided to keep running the bed and breakfast. Only now, the bookshelves were full of interesting relics and photos, and business was booming. Best of all, Molly got to feed and coddle hosts of new guests...including Griff. The fact that she'd found love late in life was better than any treasure, but having both sure didn't hurt.

Fallyn and Shaw had moved to a modestly sized house right on the ocean a few months earlier and now lived within walking distance of Molly and Griff. The four of them had dinner together every Sunday, along with the fifth member of their treasure-hunting party, Gabe, and his family. Gabe had returned to doing boat tours within days of their discovery out of sheer love for being on the water. They spent at least a few hours of their Sunday meal talking about future treasure hunts, more for fun and adventure than for enrichment.

Things were easier for Fallyn and Shaw now, but they went about their day to day in much the same way as they had. They'd moved out of Shaw's office space and were now working from home, but they were still both investigating cases every day. There was a beautiful freedom in being able to seek out stories that moved them, regardless of whether they were getting paid to do it. She and Shaw had already solved two cold cases that had brought closure for the victims' families and had several more in the works. When Anna Sullivan mentioned the Wren Hazelton kidnapping at the Sullivan family's Thanksgiving dinner, they'd dropped everything and made the drive to Cherry Blossom Point. Helping solve crimes of the past was fulfilling, but this?

This was different.

They actually had a chance to use their skills to affect the outcome for little Wren and her family.

Shaw laid a comforting arm on her shoulder as they stepped up to the doorway, and she let out a long breath.

They had already set up an interview with the father, Graham Hazelton, in an hour, and would only have time to drop off their things before they had to leave.

Before they could reach for the knob, the door swung open, revealing a rosy-cheeked, chestnut-haired woman around Fallyn's age who shot them a grin.

"Welcome! I'm Eleanor Petty, but you can just call me Ellie," she said, dipping her head in greeting. Fallyn and David made their introductions, and the woman continued, "I, er—I hope you enjoy your stay here, and you can let me know if you need anything. I understand you're a little short on time right now, so I won't keep you any longer. Let me show you to your room."

They followed the woman through the house, and Fallyn found herself relieved at how neat and well put together the place was. It was an older home, yet every surface was clean enough to eat off of, and it was beautifully decorated, with shells and flowery paintings with color palettes that suited the rooms perfectly. The bed and breakfast hadn't been in business very long, but Ellie clearly knew what she was doing when it came to creating a comfortable atmosphere.

"Right here," Ellie said, pushing one of the doors open to reveal a pristine room painted in seafoam green.

"The whole place is so beautiful," Fallyn said as she stepped into the room. They'd be spending a lot of time working on the case, but it'd be nice to have a comfortable space to come back to at the end of the day.

"I'm happy you like it," Ellie said, cheeks flushing slightly. She shifted a little. "Well... I'll let you get to it as I've got to get started on dinner."

"Thanks so much," David said, rolling their suitcase over to the single dresser in the corner.

As the woman walked away, Fallyn was already shifting back into work mode.

"We can unpack when we get back," she murmured absently. "Let's just go over things one more time. Initial thoughts so far: The six-year-old daughter of a wealthy House Representative disappeared from her bed the night before Thanksgiving without a trace. Not a crime of opportunity or impulse. They knew where she lived, where her room was, that she was at her mother's that night. This was clearly planned with Wren as the target. Seems quite possible it's a ransom thing, you think?"

Shaw nodded. "It *is* a little strange that they'd have kept her for a couple of days without contacting the family for said ransom, but I sure hope that's what it is. Graham is one of the richest men in town, so he'd be an obvious target."

"Can't rule out it being a personal or political vendetta, either," Fallyn commented, nibbling at the inside of her lip as she reached into her bag and pulled out a notebook and pen. "His image isn't all bad, but he's definitely divisive. Maybe someone's got a grudge."

"In that same vein, we should try to get an idea of what the rest of their family is like. Always most likely it's the work of a family member."

"The police have spent lots of time talking with the parents, and so far, they don't consider either of them suspects. That said, we can't rule out the idea that it could've been an accidental death and a cover-up out of fear of being prosecuted unjustly."

Could've been a neighbor, a trusted friend, the child's

soccer coach, or even a stranger who had seen pictures of Wren online and been obsessed. Right now, they had loads of questions and precious few answers. The nerves were really starting to set in, but she shoved them aside.

She was good at this.

No.

She was *great* at it. Her gut instincts had never let her down. She just had to believe in herself and Shaw and maintain hope that there was still a chance to save Wren.

She shut her notebook and dropped it back into her purse before looking up at Shaw with a grim smile.

"Let's see if Graham Hazelton can shed some light on things for us, shall we?"

Ellie's Bed and Breakfast had been lovely, but Graham Hazelton's house put it—along with basically every other house Fallyn had seen in person—to shame. As they pulled into the circular driveway, Fallyn marveled at the size of and grandeur of the place. The grounds were stunning, despite the cold of winter, and the work truck parked in the driveway touted *Quality lawn care for quality people!* She and Shaw headed up the long walkway, and she let out a low whistle at the massive door as they approached. Flanked by two Mount Olympus-worthy columns, it looked like the entrance to a famous cathedral instead of a family home.

It was just a moment later when she was able to confirm that the inside was even nicer than the outside. They trailed behind the male housekeeper who'd greeted them at the door, and Fallyn's eyes wandered as they walked. From a huge grandfather clock to a half-dozen antique shelves packed to the gills with treasures, it was nothing short of a marvel. The most consistent feature, however, were the framed photographs of a beautiful young woman that adorned nearly every wall. If Fallyn hadn't already seen a picture of her as they'd researched, she might have wondered for a brief moment whether the Congressman had another, older daughter. No, this lovely young specimen was his wife, Maura.

"Right this way," the housekeeper said, rapping twice on the first closed door they'd come to before pulling it open with a flourish.

Graham Hazelton rose to meet them as they entered, shaking each of their hands as the door swung shut behind them. He was a tall man with strong features and brown hair peppered with just enough silver to offer a sense of gravitas and wisdom.

"Glad to meet you both, and thank you for coming," he said, gesturing for them to sit in the two chairs on the near side of his desk. "I read about some of your work in Bluebird Bay, and I must admit, it has me feeling much more hopeful about our chances of finding my little Wren. While our police department is fine for small-town issues, I can't help but think they're in over their head here." He took his own seat across from them, shaking his head sadly as he glanced at the small framed photograph next to his closed laptop screen.

It was tilted at an angle that let Fallyn see it as well, and her breath caught for the briefest of moments as she caught sight of a little girl's gap-toothed, smiling face. Wren's strawberry blond curls shone in the sunlight, and she looked as happy and carefree as a child her age should. Far from the way she'd be feeling now, Fallyn knew, and the thought gutted her.

She took in a deep inhale, shifting her attention back to the matter at hand. Thinking about the what ifs would only muddy the waters. She was a professional, and the best way she could help Wren right now was to stay focused on the task at hand and get every shred of information she could out of this meeting.

"We trust the Cherry Blossom PD to do a thorough job and plan to make sure we don't get in their way. As with any small town with limited resources for these types of crimes, though, we firmly believe a second set of capable hands can only help," David said. "I'm sorry to make you repeat this all again, but the sooner we can get caught up, the sooner we can get to work."

He nodded. "Of course. I can help you with whatever you need."

Fallyn pulled out her recorder along with a notebook and pen. The latter because it helped solidify things in her mind to write them down, the former just in case she forgot anything. She'd done this countless times before, and her interview skills had always been one of her greatest strengths. Time to put them to use for something good.

"I'd like to start by getting an overall background on Wren's daily life, her schedule, and that type of thing if that's alright. I understand that you and her mother are divorced. Could you tell me a bit more about that?"

"Sure," he said with a nod. "Alicia and I got divorced three years ago. She can be emotional sometimes, but she is a good woman and loves Wren a lot. I just... We just didn't feel that our lives were headed in the same direction anymore. I'd decided at that point that I wanted to be a career politician, and she wasn't cut out to be a potential first lady in waiting, so to speak."

Fallyn digested that tidbit slowly, reading between the lines. So the Congressman was basically insinuating that he had big political ambitions, and his ex-wife didn't support them. Yet something told Fallyn that it was more like he wanted to be president someday, and his new wife was younger, prettier, and made for a better Instagram post on his arm during campaign season.

"And was the divorce amicable?"

Something flickered in his eyes and then disappeared as he shifted slightly in his chair. "As much as these types of things can be, yes. Alicia's main concern was ensuring she had primary custody of Wren. I was okay with that because my work is very demanding. I have visitation one weekend a month, as well as some holidays and a couple weeks in the summers. I was due to have Wren Thanksgiving night, but then–" His fist curled into a ball as he broke off and shook his head bitterly. "Sorry. It's just...I should've spent more time with her. I told myself it was all I could manage with my political commitments and such."

"It's tough for any parent to find that work-life balance," Fallyn replied, feeling a pang of sympathy for the man as she scribbled down his words in shorthand. "So she's with Alicia the majority of the time. Any grandparents, babysitters?"

Graham shook his head. "She stays with her aunt, Alicia's sister, once in a while, but mostly with her mother, yes. Alicia wasn't big on strangers watching Wren much."

"Speaking of strangers, how about anyone walking by the house too often, or maybe someone at the park without a child? Can you think of any strange interactions that might not have seemed significant at the time?"

He pursed his lips for a long moment and shrugged. "I don't often...that is, typically Wren and I don't spend much time at the park or places like that. We do watch movies together in our home theater from time to time and share meals when she's here, though," he rushed to assure her.

She scratched that down, keeping her expression neutral, and then looked up and held Graham's gaze.

"Mr. Hazelton, I have to say, it seems like a distinct possibility that Wren may have been a target due to your position," Fallyn continued. "I'm sure you meet a lot of people, but is there anyone who stands out as a potential enemy? Anyone you can think of who'd have a motive to do something like this?"

He nodded grimly. "I've been considering that too and gave a list to the police yesterday. I'll have my secretary make a copy of it for you to take on your way out. I have to warn you, though, it's a pretty lengthy document. I wanted to be thorough, and politics is a messy game. People are willing to go to astonishing lengths to get a leg up. I don't want to point fingers, but coming into an election year, anything is possible."

"It'll give us something to start with, at least," Shaw interjected. "Could you mark any of them you think might be more promising than the others?"

Graham nodded. "I tried to put them in order of most to least likely. And again, long shots, most likely, but I want to make sure you have anything at all that might be of help."

"Excellent, we appreciate that," Fallyn said, scanning the information she'd collected so far.

There was a sharp rap at the door behind them, and Fallyn turned to see a trim woman in a pantsuit poking her head through the open door.

"Sorry to interrupt, sir. I just wanted to make sure you didn't forget about your 7:00 reservation at La Sicilia."

Anger flashed in his eyes as he looked at her and then glanced at the clock. When he turned back to face Fallyn, he managed an apologetic smile. "Right, I'm sorry to cut this short, but I do have to get ready to go."

Fallyn blinked. He was going out for high-end Italian food while his daughter was missing? A wave of confusion ran through her, and it must've shown on her face.

"We can talk again tomorrow if need be, but we're going to be meeting with a small group to discuss some potential new climate measures. As much as I want the world to stop spinning until we find our little Wren, my responsibility to my constituents never ceases, even in a crisis." He glanced at her a moment longer, then pressed on, "And me making appearances, keeping myself and Wren in the public eye and staying at the forefront of people's thoughts is critical. I bet half the state of Maine would recognize Wren if they saw her by now."

Fallyn nodded slowly. "I understand. It makes sense."

And in a way, it kind of did. But there was something that rubbed her the wrong way about the man. She didn't have any reason to hate Graham Hazelton. But she sure as hell didn't like him.

"Helen, can you make them a copy of that list we made for the police and anything else they need?" Graham asked, turning his attention to the secretary as he gathered his things to go.

"Of course," she said, turning to Fallyn and David. "My office is one door down; we can go grab it now."

"Thanks a lot," Fallyn said a few minutes later, as Helen handed her the promised list.

"Sure," the woman said, locking eyes with her before looking away. After a moment of silence, she said, "We're so broken up about this. I just...I'm praying for you and that little girl. She's a sweet one. If you have anything else you wanted to ask Mr. Hazelton, I could write it down for you and get some answers back to you by tomorrow morning."

Fallyn met David's eyes, shrugging. "We'll let you know, thank you."

They said their goodbyes and headed back to the car.

"First impressions?" Shaw asked as he fished through his pocket for his keys.

"Honestly? I don't like the cut of his jib. Something just seemed a bit off about him, like he was a little too put together. And did you notice there wasn't a single picture of Wren except the one in his office?"

David nodded, starting the car. "Yet the place was practically wallpapered with photos of his new wife."

"Not a toy or drawing in sight," Fallyn noted. "But I'd guess they run a pretty tight ship, judging by how neat it was. And I have to keep reminding myself that he *is* a politician, so it does kind of make sense that he'd be able to force himself to be 'on' in that way. I will say that when I asked about visitation, he did seem to genuinely feel guilty that he hadn't spent more time with his daughter."

"Agree. That did seem genuine, and he definitely seems like a bit of a jerk, but I'm trying not to judge him too harshly just yet," David said. "People act in strange ways during crisis."

"Hopefully we'll get more from the mother when we see her tomorrow," Fallyn said, then glanced at the list of a dozen or so names they'd been given.

Or maybe one of these leads would show some promise. She just hoped that something popped for them, and soon. In cases like this, time was of the essence.

We're looking for you, Wren. Don't give up hope.

7

ANDREA

Dear Andy,

Without going too much into the details... I lost myself for a while, and I let down the people who love me so many times. I'm feeling stable again and it's been a while since I slipped up so bad, but I don't know how to apologize for the stuff I put my family through. Sorry feels like such a weak word, especially when you've said it as many times as I have. What can I say to them that's deeper and more meaningful than another apology?

Sincerely,

SOOO Sorry

Dear Sorry,

There's a beautiful old practice in Hawaii called Ho'oponopono. It's hard to translate, but it means something like 'to make good and tidy up.' It has to do with restitution and forgiveness—putting things right again. The modern version goes something like this:

I'm sorry. Please forgive me. Thank you. I love you.

You've already done the second hardest part, which is admitting that you were wrong. You've apologized. If you haven't expressed your gratitude and love, now's the time.

And the hardest part, Sorry? The part that comes after the apology? You show them every day that you meant what you said. You don't mess up the same way again. When you inevitably do mess up again in a new way, as we all do, back to basics:

I'm sorry. Please forgive me. Thank you. I love you.

Show them the same unfailing support that they've given you, and eventually it will even out.

Sincerely,

Andy

Andrea stood and stretched. Her last letter of the day was done, and Jeffrey was with Wyatt and Jack for the weekend. She went rummaging through the fridge for some lunch and settled on a leftover scoop of shepherd's pie. Just as she was sitting down to her delicious reheated mush, her phone rang. It was an unknown number, but local, so Andrea picked up.

"Hello?"

"Your car should be ready around four o'clock," a gravelly voice announced without preamble.

For a beat, she was confused. "Cole?"

"Yep."

"Um, wow. Okay. I thought—That was fast, thank you." Andrea cleared her throat, squashing the instant anxiety that rose in her chest. "What do I owe you?"

"Two fifty."

"Two hundred and fifty dollars?" Andrea was shocked. She had just been hoping the cost would be under four digits, but this... "Does that include the rental car?"

"Loaner was on the house. Managed to get a part from the junkyard good as new, and it didn't take me long to fix her up."

"Wow. Thank you. I really appreciate it."

He grunted in acknowledgement. "We close at five."

"Noted," Andrea said, glancing at the clock.

Cole hung up without saying goodbye, and Andrea sat there staring at her phone for a moment, feeling strangely guilty.

He could have charged her triple that and she wouldn't have blinked. Maybe she shouldn't have judged him as harshly as she had. So maybe his people skills were lacking. He was an honest man.

A quote from her favorite book sprang to mind.

"I certainly have not the talent which some people possess, of conversing easily with those I have never seen before. I cannot catch their tone of conversation, or appear interested in their concerns, as I often see done."

Maybe, like her lifelong literary love Fitzwilliam Darcy, Cole was just socially inept.

Andrea was prepared to admit it when she was wrong, and she had judged her new mechanic too harshly. She poked thoughtfully at her food and checked the time. She was here in Cherry Blossom Point for the foreseeable future, and good mechanics were hard to come by. More than that, she felt bad for having judged him so quickly.

She could almost hear her father's voice in her ear just like when she was younger.

"So what do we do when we're wrong?"

"We make it right, Dad," she murmured under her breath.

She would apologize and offer her thanks and gratitude, just like she'd counseled in her latest advice column.

A few hours later, Andrea walked into Cole's business with a still-warm, freshly made apple pie in hand and a belly full of crow. She had switched out her flour-dusted, formless writing attire for a scoop-neck sweater and her favorite pair of jeans and even put on a touch of makeup.

Surely apologies went over better if it looked like some effort went into them.

Starla the receptionist was at the front desk, and she narrowed her eyes suspiciously at Andrea's outfit and then the pie. The girl's makeup was lighter today, but her piercings seemed to have tripled. Her long-sleeved shirt was made of black lace that fit her like a second skin.

"Who's that for?"

"It's for Cole." Andrea shifted her purse strap on her shoulder, feeling self-conscious beneath the young woman's scrutiny. "A thank you for getting my car done so quickly."

Starla's lips tipped into a smirk. "Ha. People don't usually bring Cole's cranky ass baked treats."

Andrea chuckled. "I'm not surprised."

Starla's appraising gaze moved from the apple pie to Andrea's face. "Most people just don't get him." She tossed her glossy black hair over one shoulder. "Not like I do."

"I don't know if I really 'get' him." She glanced at the door to the garage and then back to Starla. "But he seems honest, and I'm grateful to get my car back so soon. I've had some bad experiences with mechanics in the past, and I was nervous. My dad took care of my car for years, and this is the first time in ages I've had to go it alone. Despite his lack of people skills, Cole sort of renewed my faith in the profession. So... yeah. I figured I'd bring his cranky ass a pie."

The door swung open just as she finished her little explanation, and Cole's gaze settled heavily on Andrea. His dark eyes flicked down to the apple pie and back up to her face.

"It's not often that you overhear yourself getting insulted by someone bringing you a pie," he drawled. "Makes me wonder if I should eat it."

Andrea's cheeks went hot. "You, um, missed the good part. I really appreciate the loaner car and the quick turnaround. So. No poison, I promise." She handed over the pie. "It's my dad's recipe. I wouldn't want to do anything to ruin it. It's apple."

"I like apple." There was a sudden and unexpected warmth in Cole's deep voice. It was subtle, but it was there. "My uncle used to own an orchard, so it was a staple in our house. Reminds me of being young."

Weird to imagine Cole had been a child once. Part of her had sort of assumed he'd come out of the womb a fully grown, crotchety misanthrope.

"I hope you're not bored of pie after Thanksgiving." Andrea's nerves were buzzing in a way that didn't make sense, and she had to work to keep her voice steady.

Cole shrugged. "Didn't have any. It's just me, and I don't do much for Thanksgiving these days."

Andrea watched him walk around the counter and slide the pie into a small fridge behind the reception desk. She wondered if his reason for not doing anything for

Thanksgiving was the same as hers, if it was grief that made him so gruff.

"And since I work with him and I'm the one printing out this tiny little invoice," Starla said lightly, "you probably want me to have a fat slice too?"

"There had better be at least half a pie left by the time I get to it," Cole growled in warning.

Starla swatted playfully at his arm. "I was kidding. You know I don't eat gluten."

Cole gave Andrea a beleaguered look, and she pressed her lips together to suppress a smile. She pulled a credit card out of her purse and handed it to Starla to swipe.

"Keys to the loaner?" Starla asked as Andrea signed the receipt.

"Here you go," Andrea said, handing them over. "I just have to grab my laptop from the backseat."

She headed back outside to the Subaru to get her computer bag and was doing one last check to make sure she hadn't forgotten anything when a flash of color caught her eye. She reached under the seat and pulled out a small, fuzzy, hot-pink sock.

Someone must've lost it when–

She stopped breathing as some jagged, half-remembered thing flickered to life in her mind. With a quick glance over her shoulder, she tugged out her phone and did a quick search. A flash later, the information she'd been seeking stared back at her.

For a second, she stood frozen in place, stunned.

Wren Hazelton had been wearing Little Mermaid fleece pajamas and fuzzy, hot pink socks the night she'd gone missing.

She swallowed hard and took a close up photo of the sock before shoving the phone back into her coat pocket with a shaky hand.

Don't jump to conclusions, Andrea, she counseled herself. Look what happened last time she'd done that. She wound up having to make an apology pie.

Besides, tons of kids had fuzzy pink socks. It was winter in Maine. And this was a loaner car, after all. Sure, Cole had said he'd been using it recently, but a dozen families had probably borrowed it in the past couple of months. And she'd already confirmed that Cole had a pretty solid moral compass...at least, when it came to his work. Not to mention that he had been Jack Merrill's mechanic for years and a trusted citizen of Cherry Blossom Point.

She turned the bit of fluff over in her hand, remembering a case that had made the news when Jeffrey was just a toddler. The man who had kept a teenage girl prisoner in a shed for years, teaching Sunday school all the while, beloved by his friends and neighbors. She had watched a documentary about it a few years back... *A Wolf in Sheep's Clothing.*

"Stop it, you wacko," she murmured under her breath.

She stuffed the sock back where she'd found it and locked up the loaner car before transferring her stuff back over to her own vehicle. She couldn't call the cops over a freaking sock. She needed to get in her car and go home.

Instead, her feet led her back inside.

"Forget something?" Starla asked as Andrea walked in. She had one hand in her shoulder bag, packing up to leave for the day.

"I just had a quick question for Cole." Andrea walked

through to the garage before Starla could say anything. He was wiping his hands on a dirty rag, and she didn't give herself time to think things through before blurting, "So what are you doing after this?"

She saw a glimmer of surprise in those dark eyes as he cocked his head to the side. "I'm headed home to eat that apple pie for dinner."

Andrea swallowed her fear and nodded. "Cool. Need someone to share it with? I'm new in town and don't know hardly any other adults here, so I just thought we could hang out for a little bit maybe. If that's alright..."

For a long, uncomfortable moment, she held her breath as she waited for Cole to reply. He didn't break eye contact as he stared at her, stone-faced.

Just when she was ready to cut bait and run, he cleared his throat. "Well, I have to take a shower before I eat and—"

"No problem at all," she assured him shrilly. "While you're, um, showering, I can just heat up the pie, cut us a couple slabs..."

Snoop around your house.

He looked like he was going to protest further but then just shrugged. "Sure. Okay, fine."

Not exactly an enthusiastic "yes!" but whatever. Cole Spivey didn't seem to do enthusiasm.

At least he'd agreed.

"You lead the way, and I'll follow you in my car, if that works?"

He let out a grunt which she took as an affirmative.

They were on the road a few minutes later, Andrea following Cole's car through the growing twilight. At every stop sign, she felt tempted to make a U-turn and haul ass for home. Then she thought of that tiny, fuzzy sock, and she gripped the wheel tighter.

Just weeks before, two people had risked life and limb to save her son. Without their brave actions, Jeffrey would surely be dead. Now she was potentially in a position to return the favor and help figure out what happened to Wren Hazelton. She couldn't turn her back. Not if there was a chance she could help bring that precious little girl home safe.

But as she followed Cole Spivey up the dark walkway to his home, she couldn't help but wonder if she'd made a terrible mistake...

8

FALLYN

FALLYN LEANED into David as she sucked in a breath of the late autumn breeze. A dozen thoughts at once fought for her attention as they stepped out of the car in front of Alicia Hazelton's modest white house. It was a quarter the size of her ex-husband's, and Fallyn was struck by the contrast. It was a good sign that they'd been able to get an interview with Alicia on such short notice, but that did little to calm her nerves.

They'd had all day to research as well as go over the list of names Graham had given them, and a preliminary search had left her with more questions than answers. Most of the people he'd cited as possible suspects were past and present political opponents, known zealots from the opposing political party, or people he'd had business dealings with in the past. Despite his insistence, Fallyn just couldn't get her head around the idea that someone would kidnap a child over politics or a real estate deal falling through. Then again, if her previous life as an investigative journalist had taught her anything, it was that people were capable of monstrous things.

She'd also had to check her personal distaste for Graham Hazelton. There was nothing pointing to him being involved. Most times, kidnapping by a parent occurred because they wanted to punish the other parent or because they felt they'd been shafted by either them or the system and wanted more time with the child. The Congressman had been honest about the custody agreement, and public documents proved that the divorce had gone quickly and was largely uncontested aside from some financial negotiations. If Graham had wanted custody of Wren or even more visitation, there was no record of it.

Basically, they were still sitting at square one.

They'd tried to get an early morning appointment with the little girl's mother, but her appointment with a detective on the case had taken precedence. It was nearly dinner time as they headed up the cobblestone pathway, and the clock never stopped ticking. With each passing hour, Wren's return would become less and less likely, a fact that threatened to crush Fallyn under its weight.

"We're just getting started, babe. This is the house Wren was taken from, and her mother is the person she spent most time with," David reassured her, as if in response to her thoughts. "It's very likely we'll get some good leads. Let's try to stay optimistic."

She nodded into his shoulder, letting out a sigh as they stepped onto the porch. The door swung open before they could knock, revealing a curly-haired woman who looked strikingly similar to the photograph of little Wren Hazelton that Fallyn had seen on Graham's desk. Her green eyes contrasted sharply with that same strawberry blond hair, but her cheeks were pale and lifeless.

"Thank you for coming," she said, flashing a ghost of a smile that didn't reach her eyes. She stepped aside, gesturing for them to follow after her.

"Thanks for agreeing to speak with us," Shaw replied, giving Fallyn's shoulder a squeeze and gesturing for her to step into the house before him.

The living room was only a few steps to their left, and the difference between the woman's house and Graham's was even more striking now that they were inside. It wasn't a dump by any means, but the décor was modest and sparse, the furniture worn.

Fallyn stepped around a miniature dollhouse as they moved into the dining room. Perhaps an even starker difference, however, were the framed photographs of Wren that peppered the walls of the house. From pictures of her as a newborn to ones of her standing triumphantly on a boulder in a wooded area, it was clear that this was a woman whose life revolved around her little girl. Or at least that was the impression she wanted to give.

"You can take a seat here. Can I get either of you anything to drink?" Alicia asked, her expression blank as she gestured toward the dining room table. "Water? Tea?"

"No thanks," Fallyn said, grabbing her recorder and notebook.

Shaw said the same, and the woman sat down across from them. She let out a long sigh, then nodded.

"I don't mean to be rude, but I'm just so, so tired." She threw up both hands, blinking back the sudden tears in her eyes. "What can I tell you that I haven't already said a hundred times?"

Empathy made Fallyn's stomach ache, but she pushed past it. "I know it's exhausting and frustrating, but because we're hearing it from you for the first time, why don't we start with the day of Wren's disappearance?" she said, pressing the record button. "Sometimes we find that the tiniest detail can be absolutely crucial. We wouldn't ask if we didn't have to."

The woman squeezed the bridge of her nose for a long moment before speaking. "I, um... I put Birdie down around 8:30 like usual. I was watching television in my bedroom until falling asleep at eleven or so. I woke up shivering and felt a draft coming from down the hall. When I went into her room, I found that the window was wide open and she was–" She broke off and cleared her throat. "She was gone."

Birdie.

Her mom called the little girl Birdie. Fallyn had to blink back her own tears as she jotted that down.

"And that was at what time?" she managed.

"Four-thirty or so. When I looked at the clock a few minutes later, it was four-thirty-six."

"Was Birdie's door open or did you open it?" Fallyn asked, adopting the nickname in hopes of creating a sense of trust and comfort with her mother.

"It was shut. I opened it."

"And the house was already cold when you got out of bed?" Shaw asked.

"Yes. Cold enough to wake me," Alicia said.

Fallyn nodded, making note of that. With just the one window open and the girl's bedroom door closed, it would've taken some time to cool the house, even though it was small. Likely a couple of hours.

"Do you think she could've opened the window and climbed out herself?" Fallyn already knew the answer but wanted to get Alicia into a comfortable rhythm of responding to the easy questions to pave the way to the more difficult ones.

"She wouldn't. Besides, none of her shoes were missing, and the police found one set of tracks in the snow. Large boot prints outside the window. They estimate a size eleven, but some of the snow had melted by morning, so..."

Fallyn took those notes and then shifted gears. "Was there anything strange about that night that you remember?"

"Nothing at all," the woman said, her voice sounding strangled. "That's the thing, you know? It was so *normal*. And then this..."

Fallyn had called in a favor to their detective friend in Bluebird Bay, Ethan, who had gotten a copy of the police report. The neighbors hadn't heard or seen anything, and the cops had been canvassing houses in the neighborhood to see if anyone had a camera set up that might've had the road in view, but nothing had come of it yet.

"How about the days or weeks leading up to the kidnapping?" Shaw interjected. "Did she seem nervous or more quiet than usual? Trouble sleeping, nightmares, that sort of thing?"

The woman's eyes filled with tears as she shook her head. "No. She was funny and sassy, and she hid her green beans under a carton in the trash after dinner thinking I wouldn't notice...no. She didn't seem nervous. She just seemed like...Birdie."

Fallyn nodded. "And there's no one obvious who stands out as a suspect, right? No creepy cousins who made you skittish, or a friend or even a stranger who showed her more interest than you maybe felt comfortable with?"

"No. No, nothing like that. I did have a great uncle, but he's long dead. I was very vocal with her about boundaries. If she was around family members who expected hugs and kisses at the holidays, I always told her she was in charge of her body, and if she didn't feel like hugging, she didn't have to. She also knew not to talk to strangers. I've wracked my brain thinking of anyone who stood out, but..." She shrugged helplessly.

"I'm sure you've thought of nothing else over the past three days. Do you have any theories of your own about what might have happened? Even if they seem unlikely. Anything at all, we want to hear it," Shaw encouraged.

Alicia held up both hands again in helpless surrender. "Not a theory so much, but I do keep praying we'll get a call. Like maybe a ransom thing? Her father isn't well-liked in some circles. He has an obscene amount of money, and he's not afraid to flash it around. I just don't know."

Fallyn caught up her note-taking, considering where to take the conversation next, then spoke again.

"How about enemies? We got a list of some from Graham, but it could be helpful if you could think of any he might've missed...his or yours."

Alicia opened her mouth to reply but was interrupted by a loud whooshing sound.

"Leesh? You okay?" a worried female voice called from the doorway.

"I'm fine, come on in, Lin," Alicia called in response.

"Sorry, I just saw the car in the driveway and got a little worried," the other woman said as she stepped into the room, arms loaded with Tupperware containers.

"I'm just doing a quick interview," Alicia explained, gesturing toward Fallyn and Shaw.

The women were far from identical–Alicia was a bit thinner, her hair worn long, and the other woman looked to be a few years older–but there was a strong enough resemblance that it was obvious they were sisters.

"They're those two private detectives that Graham brought in to find Birdie," Alicia said. "Fallyn Rappaport and David Shaw." She turned back toward them. "This is my sister Linda."

"Nice to meet you," Linda said, dipping her head in greeting, but the tightening of her jaw belied her words.

"Graham actually didn't bring us in. We're here pro bono," Fallyn interjected with a half-smile.

"Oh," Alicia said, eyes widening slightly. "In an interview I saw on television earlier today, he made it sound like he brought the two of you in..."

David shook his head. "Nope, we came of our own accord when we heard about Wren's disappearance. Graham was just the first person we managed to make direct contact with, and he agreed to talk to us. We don't work for him."

Alicia visibly relaxed at this news, letting out a short breath.

"Who does that?" Linda demanded with a snort of disgust. "Who would even think to take credit for hiring PIs when their kid is missing? More political gamesmanship."

Fallyn couldn't help but agree. Something seemed... gross about the white lie. Was he thinking of optics and personal gain, even in a situation like this? She'd interacted with politicians a fair number of times over her career as a journalist, though, and it definitely didn't seem out of the realm of possibility. Still, it didn't win him any points in her book. And clearly sister Linda was *not* a fan.

Linda turned to Alicia. "Leesh, I know it's tough, but you really need to get some food in you. I brought you some chicken cutlets and macaroni salad. Will you eat at least a few bites please?"

Alicia sighed, nodding. "Yeah, thanks. I'll have it when I'm finished with the interview, okay?"

"Feel free to eat now while we talk," David encouraged gently. "Don't worry about us. We've just eaten."

It was a lie, but a well-intentioned one. If poor Alicia Hazelton could find a window of time where she could stomach food, she should take it. Judging by her hollowed-out cheeks, she'd been getting about as much nourishment as she had sleep.

Alicia opened her mouth to respond, but her sister popped open the first container, setting it in front of her and saying, "Here, let me get you a fork."

Alicia shrugged, seemingly resigned. "Sure, okay."

"I'm happy enough with that, so I'll get out of your hair now," Linda said as she returned. "Sorry for the interruption, and thanks for what you two are doing to find our Birdie."

Our Birdie.

Not strange, really. If the child was close with her aunt, it made sense that she would feel some sense of ownership. Like they were *both* suffering her loss. But could Linda have taken Birdie from the home to protect her from something or someone?

Maybe from Graham? Birdie *was* due for her monthly visit when she'd been taken.

Fallyn jotted down that question in her notepad before looking up again.

"Actually, Linda," she cut in, "do you have a few minutes? You've spent time with Wren and might be able to offer some insight."

She shrugged, lowering herself into an empty chair. "Sure."

Fallyn glanced back to her notebook as Alicia took a tentative bite of her food.

"Okay, so we were talking about enemies. Anyone that sticks out?" If there were any names that overlapped with the list Graham had given them, maybe they could narrow their focus some.

Linda let out a bark of laughter. "Where do we start? To know Graham Hazelton is to despise him. I can definitely see someone mowing him down on the street," she said with a callous shrug, "but to involve a child? To drag an innocent, sweet little girl into it like our Birdie?" She shook her head, swiping a tear from the corner of her eye. "I just don't see it."

Alicia swallowed carefully before interjecting. "I have to agree. Graham can be... deceitful. He makes a lot of big promises, and he's not known for following up on them. At least when it comes to people who know him well."

More words than she's spoken all night, Fallyn thought. Perhaps she'd been wary when she thought they were here on Graham's behalf and more trusting now that they knew the truth.

She said a silent prayer of thanks for sister Linda's intrusion.

"There are those who would want to punish him," Alicia continued, "but anyone who knows him knows this is far more of a blow to me than to Graham. They'd have been better off hitting him where it counts." Her eyes went chilly. "Right in the campaign."

That was a pretty brutal statement to make, and Fallyn's lingering questions about whether the divorce had been truly amicable fizzled away.

Alicia perched her fork on the edge of the Tupperware and settled back against her seat. "Granted, I haven't spent much time around him since the divorce, but I doubt that would've changed, especially since he's only gotten more powerful over the years."

"Could you tell us a little bit about that? The divorce and the aftermath?" Fallyn asked, taking advantage of the opening. It was important to piece together all they could about Wren's family life. It seemed odd that Alicia lived this modestly after divorcing such a wealthy man. Or perhaps she was just living below her means.

"The separation was brutal on me at first," Alicia admitted, crossing her arms over her chest as if she'd caught a chill. "I...I, um, started drinking a good bit. I was still able to care for Birdie, but it was an issue. Initially, he asked me for a fifty-fifty split, using my mental state, the drinking, and some lies he made up about me as a justification." She bit at her cheek, shaking her head. "His new wife Maura was his girlfriend at the time, and she liked the idea of having Birdie around for the first few months. Liked dressing her up like a doll, getting family photo ops, all of it."

"And I think *he* loved the optics of being an involved father," Linda interjected, a disgusted look on her face. "You should've seen the articles. Pictures of him playing with her outside, taking her to swim at the lake. He hates the outdoors. But he lives and dies by what the press thinks of him. You should've seen him a couple months ago when that whole scandal about him paying for sex using his checkbook came out." Her lips tipped into a fierce grin. "'Member, Leesh? I thought he was going to jump off a bridge when the headlines hit. More's the pity... His people managed to downplay it and drag the woman's name through the mud instead, but it was a close call. I don't know if he ever fully recovered in the polls."

She'd seen a few of those articles, and sister Linda was right. He'd gotten off pretty easy, considering. She jotted down a note on that and turned back to Alicia.

"You were saying that initially he wanted more time with her. What changed that?"

"Reality, I'm guessing. He just called me one night and offered to forget the custody stuff entirely if I would give him some favorable concessions on the financial side of things. I could've taken him to the cleaners otherwise, but having Birdie the majority of the time was more important."

"He and Maura got married a few weeks later, and she got a new bichon frise puppy. He's hardly looked at Birdie since, even on their designated weekends. Trash. Both of them," Linda practically spat.

Fallyn nodded, noting it all down and trying to stay objective. Her heart ached for Alicia, but she had to remember she was only hearing half the story and that this wasn't something that should get in the way of an honest accounting of the facts, even if it did jive with the picture she'd already mentally painted of Graham Hazelton.

"We've taken enough of your time for now, so we'll let

you have a visit and eat," Shaw said, glancing at his watch and then turning to Fallyn. "Was there anything else?"

"Alicia..." Fallyn met the other woman's gaze and held it. "Do you have any reason to believe Graham might have been...hurting Birdie in any way?"

Alicia drew back with a start. "Hurting her? Like how?" Before Fallyn could even form a reply, Alicia was shaking her head. "No. No way. He's apathetic and selfish, but he doesn't have it in him to physically harm another person. At least, I don't think he does..."

"You give him too much credit," Linda cut in. "I wouldn't put anything past him. There were several weekends when Birdie asked if she had to go there. And who could blame her? They barely paid attention to her." She looked down at her wringing hands and then looked up again. "Look, I'm not accusing him of anything. I'm just saying...I wouldn't put it past him."

Fallyn and Shaw exchanged a glance, and Fallyn nodded slowly.

"Well, ladies, we really appreciate you all talking to us. I think that's all for now, but we will definitely be in touch, if that's alright?" Fallyn said as she gathered her things and moved to stand.

"Absolutely. Give me a call if you need anything else, and please keep me in the loop," Alicia said, her eyes pleading. "Anything, any news at all, any time, day or night. And thank you again for doing all this. It truly means a lot to know there are more people looking for my Birdie."

When she and Shaw had climbed back into the car, they turned to face one another.

"I would bet Lopez's treasure Alicia had nothing to do with this," she said without preamble.

"And Linda?" Shaw asked, one brow rising quizzically.

"Her, I'm not so sure..."

Shaw turned the key in the ignition, and a moment later they were back on the road. Still armed with more questions than answers, but at least they were getting a better sense of who these people were.

She let out a long sigh, her breath a puff of white in the darkness. It was going to be another bitterly cold night, and she could only hope little Wren was somewhere safe and warm...

9

ANDREA

"I CAN TAKE YOUR COAT," Cole said as he shrugged off his own and eyed her expectantly.

Andrea just stared at him blankly, wanting with all her heart to decline the offer. If she was down to her sweater and jeans, she'd feel all that much more vulnerable, which was ludicrous.

If this mountain of a man wanted to hurt her, a layer of camel-colored Merino wool certainly wasn't going to stop him.

Besides, she'd already been off the charts on the weird-meter so far with this guy. The last thing she needed to do was add to his suspicions by insisting she leave her coat on indoors.

She stripped it off and handed it to him, shivering almost instantly.

"I usually turn the heat down to sixty during the day since I'm not home," he said as he closed the closet door, turning back to face her, "but it will get warm pretty fast once I turn up the thermostat."

She nodded agreeably, wondering if poor little Wren was in the bowels of the house somewhere, shivering too. Although, if she was being honest, this quaint little raised ranch didn't look like it had a whole lot of bowels. In fact, it looked pretty nice. The exterior had been painted a cheery shade of butter yellow and was surrounded by a well-kept lawn and nicely trimmed evergreen shrubs. And from what she could see so far, the inside was neat as a pin.

As she glanced around, she couldn't help but note the dozens of ceramic vases, trays, and pitchers filling every available space. Most were slightly misshapen and or a little off-kilter, but they all had a unique style. Almost as if they were intentionally skewed, like the teacups at a Mad Hatter party.

The place looked more like the home of a very fastidious art teacher than a kidnapper... or a mechanic, for that matter.

"Did you make these?" she marveled, leaning in to admire a squat little pot that housed a trio of colorful succulents.

He shook his head curtly. "Nope. Starla made them. She gives them to me for—well, all the time." He glanced at the piece she was studying and shrugged. "They're getting better, actually. You should see some of the early stuff. I keep most of that in the den."

The fact that he displayed them at all—and seemingly each and every one of them—struck her.

Not exactly the actions of a hard-ass grouch of a mechanic...or a kidnapper.

She cleared her throat and straightened, about to speak when a crash came from somewhere below.

She jerked back with a gasp. "What was that?"

"Jezebel," he replied, frowning. "My cat."

Likely story. Although he looked more annoyed than nervous or concerned, as one would imagine a person with something to hide might be.

"I'd better go see what she's gotten into," he continued, handing off the pie and then heading toward the stairs. "Do you mind throwing a couple slices into the oven to heat them? Once I deal with the cat, I'll take a quick shower and we can eat. I'm pretty sure I've got vanilla ice cream in the freezer that I can scoop on top."

"Sounds great," she said, forcing a smile.

When he was out of sight, she let the smile falter.

This was nuts. Surely, Cole wouldn't have allowed her into his house and left her to her own devices upstairs if Wren were nearby. The whole thing was ridiculous, and the second he came back upstairs, she was going to—

Another crash sounded, followed by a muffled oath, and goosebumps broke out on her skin. A moment later, footsteps sounded up the stairs, and she scurried toward the kitchen.

She had just managed to carve two slices from the pie when he poked his head in.

"Find everything you need?"

"Yep," she managed, despite the fact that her heart was beating out of her chest. She turned to give him a thumbs-up and froze. A crimson bead of blood trickled down his cheek. "Wh—um, what happened?" she asked, clutching her fingers around the chef's knife more tightly.

His brows caved together as he lifted a hand to his face.

"Ah, I guess the little hellion got me. I adopted her from the shelter over the summer, and we're still in the negotiation stage of deciding who's boss. I'll put some antibiotic cream on it after my shower. Be back in ten."

A moment later, he was gone, leaving her on shaking legs, knife in hand. That scratch could've been from Jezebel the cat, just like Cole had said. Or it could've been from a scared little girl seeing her chance to get away and putting up a fight.

She glanced around the perimeter of the room and frowned. There was no sign of a cat anywhere that she could see. No bowls for food and water, no kitty litter box or ball with a bell inside of it.

Nada.

"Maybe that stuff is in the bathroom or the laundry room," she muttered under her breath.

And still, she couldn't convince herself. Not after the scratch...not fully.

She set the knife down with a clatter and dug her cell phone from her pocket. Pulling up her own email address, she tapped out a quick message.

I'm fine but in the event that no one hears from me again, I'm at Cole Spivey's house.

She hit send, pocketed her phone, and then stood there, taut as a tripwire. As she waited for the sound of the running shower, she found herself holding in a bubble of semi-hysterical laughter, imagining what advice she would give to someone in her current situation.

Dear Andy,

I met a man who I have reason to believe might have kidnapped a little girl from her bed in the middle of the night.

I'm thinking I should invite myself over his house for pie so I can snoop. Thoughts?
   -Big, Stupid, Dumb Idiot in Maine

"Dear Big, I'm thinking you might want to reconsider," she murmured under her breath. "And also potentially seek therapy to get to the root of why you feel the need to put yourself in mortal peril on a hunch rather than just, you know, calling the police like a normal person."

As she looked around the room, her gaze caught on a particularly unattractive bowl that was clearly one of Starla's earlier works, and a prick of guilt poked at her.

But people were never just one thing, were they? Someone could be kind enough to display a friend's questionable art project while also being a kidnapper. The two weren't mutually exclusive. Besides, she hadn't accused him of anything. She was here solely on a recon mission. Once she assured herself that Wren Hazelton wasn't tucked away here somewhere, she'd make a decision whether to come clean and talk to Cole about what she'd found or call the police.

After what felt like an eternity, she finally heard the sound of the shower running. She gave it sixty Mississippis for good measure in case he forgot something and came back out. Then she snagged the apple-filling-coated knife and made a beeline for the stairs.

"This is so stupid." She whispered it over and over like a mantra as she crept down the steps, every nerve on high alert.

She didn't dare turn the lights on, using the moonlight streaming through the windows to guide her. The space was used as a family room, with a pair of large, overstuffed couches and a coffee table in the middle. She searched high and low, but if there was a little girl hidden somewhere, she couldn't find her. Next, she turned her attention to the little laundry room off to the side. That was when she saw the litter box along with food and water tucked up beside the dryer.

So he *did* have a cat.

This whole mission was feeling like a foolish waste of time now, but in for a penny...

She continued forward toward the door to the garage and laid a hand on the knob.

"Wren?" she called softly as she twisted. She opened the door slowly and let it swing open. "Wren Hazelton, are you in there?"

But the only thing in the garage was a bunch of tools, as far as she could tell. She closed the door and let out a long breath.

Unless he had a hidden room or secret passageway, it seemed unlikely that Cole Spivey had tucked little Wren somewhere in this house.

Now stop acting crazy, go upstairs, and heat up some pie.

"Andrea?"

She wheeled around and crashed straight into Cole's broad chest, practically bouncing off it with a muffled "Oof!"

She backed up as he steadied her with a hand on her upper arm, enveloping her in a cloud of sandalwood soap and damp man. He glanced down at the knife at her side, and his puzzled expression darkened.

"What the hell? What are you doing down here?"

Panic closed over her as she tried to think of what to say.

"Jezebel...um, she was making a racket, and I thought

maybe she needed my help. I came down and she ran behind the washer and dryer—"

As if on cue, a jet-black feline padded across the room, sat at her owner's feet, and proceeded to begin grooming herself.

Cole looked down at the cat and then back at Andrea, cocking his head. "Is that a knife in your hand?"

"A knife?" she asked with a snort. "Funny you should ask that. I suppose it *is* a knife. I guess I forgot I was holding it from when I was cutting the pie."

Cole closed the scant distance between them, only stopping when they were toe to toe. "I thought it was super odd that you invited yourself over in the first place. And now, with you standing there with that knife in your hand, I'm starting to wonder if maybe you're up to something." He paused for a long moment as his dark eyes drilled into hers. "Are you up to something, Andrea?"

She swallowed hard and shook her head, but suddenly, the stress became too much, and she wound up nodding as a confession bubbled from her lips.

"I found a pink sock in your Subaru, and it looked like the ones Wren Hazelton was wearing when she went missing, and since the car was at your house and you've been using it, I started thinking that maybe she was...that you...um, that she might be here, so I made up an excuse to come to your house and check, and then your cat started making all that noise and you came up with blood on your face and I thought... well, I think you know what I thought."

She went suddenly breathless and quiet, but he didn't make any effort to fill the void. He just stared down at her in the dim light.

84

"Cole?" she murmured, wishing there was some place to put the knife that she now felt very silly holding it.

"So your plan was, what? To rescue Wren and then stab me with my own pie knife?" he drawled.

His tone was low and even, but it felt like a sonic boom, and she wished the floor would open up and swallow her whole.

"The knife was a last minute add-on," she clarified. "I had no plan beyond checking to see if Wren was here."

He shook his head, and his lips quirked into something close to a smile.

"I gotta admit, as nutty as that all sounds, it's pretty ballsy of you. Why didn't you just call the cops?"

"I didn't want to go around pointing fingers your way without having at least some sort of credible information. For all I know, you could've killed a man in a bar fight two decades ago. The cops might've railroaded you, and this would be your second strike..."

Even as the words left her mouth, she knew they sounded almost as ridiculous as the rest of it.

The half-smile became a full-blown grin. "You sure were blessed with one hell of an imagination."

"It's why I became a writer," she admitted, face flaming. "I was never good at long-form fiction, though, so..." She trailed off and cleared her throat. "Look, I'm really sorry. I was way out of line, and then Jezebel acted up, and the plot thickened."

"It's okay. I didn't get it at first, but I get it now."

He was being very gracious about the whole thing, considering. And, in spite the overwhelming urge to turn tail, run home, and bury her head in humiliation, there was an unidentified pink sock to be dealt with.

"We've established that I obviously jumped to conclusions, but now what?" she asked, cheeks still pink from embarrassment.

"Well, I will need to look through the records to see who had this car before me. If the dates line up with when Wren was kidnapped, then we have to call the police in the event they are a suspect."

"I just don't want to make the same mistake twice and cast suspicion unjustly," she admitted sheepishly. "It's probably some other little girl's sock. I'm sure there are thousands like it in Cherry Blossom Point."

Cole nodded. "True. And if that's the case, and whoever had the loaner did nothing wrong, it won't be a big deal. No harm, no foul. But if the sock is evidence, we need to get it into the right hands."

"Okay," she agreed readily, "but I have one request."

"What's that?"

"I'd like to give Fallyn Rappaport a call first."

Cole's forehead wrinkled. "The name sounds familiar..."

"Former crack-shot investigative journalist, current PI who not only solved the cold case of Emily Addison over in Bluebird Bay, but also spearheaded the search and discovery of Lopez's gold."

Cole's expression cleared. "That's right. Hazelton hired her to work Wren's case, didn't he?"

She nodded. "And if we call the police first, they're going to take the sock, impound the car, and she'll never get a chance to see what we've got." Cole opened his mouth to respond, and she rushed to continue. "I just know that, if it was me, and my daughter was out there? I'd want the best people on the job, no stone unturned. Fallyn is a bulldog. She solved a case that hadn't been solved in decades. Found a treasure that had been missing for a century. She's the person I'd want if it was my kid."

Her pulse was pounding at the end of her little sales pitch, but dang it, she meant it. It was Cole's place of business, and if he said no, she'd respect that.

She really hoped he didn't say no, though...

"Alright. I can see you really believe in her, and my only goal is to see that kid back with her family before the holidays. Plus, I don't see the harm in it. So long as we can call the police tonight."

She bobbed her head. "Deal."

10

FALLYN

Fallyn took a long sip from her coffee, re-reading the last of her notes. Their host, Ellie, had prepared a pot of the stuff for their return, and she was thankful for it after such a long day. "Anything stand out as a place to start?"

"I think we should do a little more research into those closest to Wren before comparing the lists Graham and Alicia provided," David said, staring pensively at the ceiling.

"That makes sense," Fallyn agreed. "I still can't quite let go of the idea that Graham might have something to do with this. Any possibility he's changed his tune on the custody situation and decided to take her for himself?"

"If he changed his mind, then he kept it to himself, because Alicia didn't seem suspicious of him in that regard," Shaw replied. "In fact, she didn't seem to think he wanted her around much at all."

Fallyn frowned but nodded, taking it all in. "What if he was considering another run at custody, even just for show? Either Alicia or the aunt could've kidnapped the kid to 'protect' her from that. Especially if Linda is right, and Wren didn't like going there."

She had to keep her bias toward the mother in check, and she had to admit that the pieces *did* kind of fit. Why had she seemed so much more open after finding out they hadn't been hired by Graham? She chewed at her lip.

"Wren *did* disappear from Alicia's house without a trace. Who better to pull something like that off than the woman herself or someone she was involved with?" She mulled it over for a few more seconds, then continued, "But what would her endgame even be? It's not like she'd be able to just bring her kid back home someday like nothing happened. It seems weird."

"People do crazy things when their kids are involved," David said with a shrug. "Look, I honestly doubt either of them are the culprit, but it's probably the best path to pursue for now."

"There's still the possibility of an accidental death and a coverup," Fallyn added. "The footprints outside the window could've been staged by Alicia or even been those of a male friend helping the mom out to make it look like a kidnapping. Hell, Graham and Alicia could've done it together."

Fallyn shook her head slowly. "The police did establish that Graham's shoe size is a nine, but that doesn't really mean anything. I guess it's possible, although they don't seem to have a very good relationship."

"If Alicia was afraid of going to jail for neglect and Graham was afraid of how things might look in the polls if he waived his right to custody and his daughter was killed at his ex's home?"

"Seems thin, but it's possible," she said dubiously. "Maybe we should start with looking over the specific filings Graham made about getting custody of Wren. If those don't match what we've heard so far, that'd definitely give us something to look into."

David nodded, taking a sip from his mug of coffee before pushing his laptop open. "Good idea. Let me do a little digging."

Fallyn glanced out the window, taking in the moonlit autumn landscape as he tapped away at his keyboard. Before she had much time to ponder, her phone began to buzz audibly in her pocket.

Alicia? Maybe Graham?

She yanked it out and answered it. "Hello?"

"Hi, I-I'm Andrea Phillips, and I'm trying to reach Fallyn Rappaport," said a woman's voice she didn't recognize.

"This is she," Fallyn answered, waiting for the other woman to say more. Maybe someone with a tip about the case.

"I saw that you've been investigating the disappearance of Wren Hazelton," Andrea continued. "And I followed your work on the Emily Addison case. You were amazing." The woman paused for a long moment—so long that Fallyn almost interjected—before continuing, her voice softer and even more shaken up than before. "I was planning to take this right to the police, but I thought I should call you first."

"Okay, I'm listening." Shaw looked up in question, but Fallyn put up a finger, mouthing, *One second.*

"I'm at a mechanic's shop on Chestnut Street, and I—I think I may've stumbled across something related to the crime. One of the loaners had a sock in the back seat that matches the description of the socks Wren Hazelton was wearing when she was taken. Once I call the police, they likely won't let you in to look, and I just want to make sure that we have all hands on deck looking for Wren. If you want to come now, I can hold off on contacting the police for half an hour while the owner of the shop does some research on who might've been driving the car."

Fallyn's heart skipped a beat, and the mix of anxiety and anticipation must've shown on her face, because David stepped away from his laptop, leaning down to hear.

"My partner and I can come by right away. What's the address?"

Andrea told her, and Fallyn hung up the phone, turning to David.

"We've got to go. Apparently, a sock like the Wren was wearing was found in the back seat of a loaner car at a local mechanic's shop."

David's eyes widened. "Anything else that seems promising?"

"That's all she saw as far as I know, but maybe we'll see something she missed."

Shaw glanced at his computer, then back to her. "We should try to make the best of our time here. Why don't you go and I can stay and finish the rest of this background check on Alicia? Just take plenty of pictures."

Yet another thing she loved about David Shaw. He trusted her to do her job right and had no BS toxic ideas about having to be "the man" and do all the important work himself. A true partnership that she had only dreamed of.

"Good luck," he said, leaning in to kiss her forehead. "This could be an important breakthrough."

He pulled away and went back to his laptop as she grabbed her coat and headed out the door.

There was a twinge of anxiety in the back of Fallyn's mind as she pulled into the parking lot of the mechanic's shop a short while later. There were a few cars spread throughout, but there didn't seem to be any actual people around.

"Hey," a voice called loudly, and her fears were lessened when she saw a woman around her age stepping through the door of the shop, waving her lit-up phone above her head. A large man stepped out behind her, waving as well.

This would be a pretty bad murder set-up, she told herself. She'd had plenty of time to share where she was going with others before leaving, after all. She patted at her pocket anyway, making sure she knew where her pepper spray was in case things took a bad turn.

She pulled up, popped the car into park in front of the door, and turned off the ignition.

"Thanks for coming. I'm Andrea, this is Cole," the woman said, gesturing toward the tall man with a serious expression beside her. "That's it there." She nodded toward the Subaru a few spaces to their left as Fallyn stepped out of her car and closed the door behind her.

"How much of it has been disturbed? Have other people used the car since the day of the kidnapping?"

"Just me and Andrea," Cole said. "I didn't use the backseat at all."

"I did put my laptop and some groceries back there, but I didn't know..."

Now that they were here in person, it was clear just how shaken up the woman was by all this. It was written all over her ashen face.

"You had no way of knowing. And if you hadn't used the back seat, we might never have found the sock. If this turns out to belong to Wren, it could be exactly the breakthrough we need to find her."

Andrea let out a shuddering breath. "You're right. Okay, thanks."

"Let's go take a look, okay?" Fallyn encouraged.

She followed Cole's lead as they made their way to the Subaru. She wouldn't want to disturb anything inside or screw up any potential evidence for the police, so she'd have to be very cautious with her inspection. She tugged out the rubber gloves she'd tucked in her pocket and pulled them on before gingerly opening the door.

"Have you looked into the records for who had this car on that day yet?" she asked, carefully examining the clean tan interior. No obvious signs of anything, except the pink sock sticking out from under the seat.

Cole made a click of annoyance. "John Weaver was the name he'd given. Could be an alias, in hindsight, and I don't collect much information besides that. I've never had a problem with someone not returning a loaner. He only had it the one day since it was just a tune-up. Starla had taken the day off, but if I recall, I'm pretty sure I left his keys in the box that night, and the loaner was back in the lot when I came to work. All pretty typical."

"Hmm," Fallyn said, leaning over to peer under the seats. Still nothing. She snapped several pictures with the flash anyway. "How about the car he brought in? Could you give me his plates and the make and model?"

"One sec." She heard footsteps behind her as the man walked away, and she looped around to the other side of the car, snapping more photos of the back seat. When Cole returned, he spoke again. "Here. Made a copy of these earlier so you can keep them for now."

She turned, accepting the papers. She glanced over them, then shot a quick text to David. *Can you look into this car for me? Apparently this is the one the suspect brought in for maintenance.* She attached a picture of the document, then got back to searching.

"I do have a camera in the parking lot, but it's been sketchy the past six months, and I haven't gotten around to replacing it. Once I looked up the info on the car and all, I was going to check and see if there was any footage."

Fallyn perked up at that. Assuming the sock did belong to Wren, video of the person driving the car would be a game-changer.

"Okay, so we can hope for that. As soon as we're done here, if you can cue up the dates he dropped off and picked up, that would be great." She turned away from Cole to face Andrea. "How'd you stumble on the sock?" Fallyn asked gently.

"I was using the loaner while Cole worked on my car, and I noticed it just when I was about to return it," Andrea answered, stepping closer to lean into the vehicle. "It was right around that same spot when I found it," she said, jabbing her finger toward the sock.

Fallyn's phone dinged before she could respond, and she unlocked it to see a text back from Shaw.

Stolen plates. Registered to an SUV a few towns over.

She read the text aloud, her heart threatening to thump out of her chest, then stood.

"We need to call the police to come have a look at this now. It'll take them a bit to get here, and I can keep poking around in the meantime, but I don't want to push it any longer than we have. You may've found the key to solving this case."

She was so focused as she continued her careful inspection that she hardly heard as Andrea made the call from behind her. Everything seemed to be basically in order, but there were still places that were difficult to see while trying to avoid touching anything. She took as many photos as possible, but doubt was beginning to creep into her mind as she scanned the ceiling spots for the dozenth time. It was as spotless as it'd been on the first look.

She took a step back, letting out an exasperated breath as she stood next to the car. *Where else was there to—?* Her breath caught in her throat, and she dropped quickly to one knee, ignoring the twinge in her leg as it met ice-cold pavement.

"Was this here before?" she asked, waving Cole over quickly and jabbing her finger at the side of the seat, where it'd meet the door when the doors were closed.

His eyes widened, and he shook his head. "Nope. No way. I get them detailed frequently, and that one was cleaned just a week before the girl went missing."

"Anything you had with you that could've left a stain like that?"

Andrea chewed at her lip and then shook her head. "I don't think so."

Fallyn unlocked her phone to text David as she stared at the rust brown splotch with growing dread. After years of crime journalism, she knew what it was with something approaching certainty.

I think we've got a blood stain.

11

ANDREA

THE POLICE HAD TAKEN their statements, confiscated the car and the video footage, and left almost twenty minutes ago, but her hands were still shaking.

Two hours had passed since they'd seen the blood, and that discovery had pushed her already overtaxed nervous system past the breaking point. Once they'd also gotten sight of the man who'd borrowed the Subaru, it had only gotten more real. He wore a knit hat and Adirondack hood pulled tight around his face, obscuring some of his features, so it wasn't much, but it was something.

The waiting room of the garage was dim, lit only through the windows by the bright lights outside, and she was glad of that. The headache building in her skull was shaping up to be a doozy.

She was alone in the room, and so she didn't feel too self-conscious as she folded in half, touched her forehead to her knees, and took a few long, deep breaths. Tears burned her eyes, but she didn't let them fall.

Not here. Not now.

Once she was home alone, curled up in her own bed... then she could let them loose, if she hadn't already pushed the feelings down too far to retrieve today.

When her hands had stopped shaking enough to manage her phone, she sat up and shot off a quick text message to Wyatt asking for an update. Jeffrey was probably asleep by now, even with the excitement of being off with his hero, but she figured Wyatt was still up. Andrea just needed reassurance that her son was okay.

She stared at her screen for a solid five minutes, bringing it back to life each time it went dark, but Wyatt didn't reply. Maybe he was asleep too. Nightmare scenarios flitted through her imagination, but she beat each one back before it could take on a life of its own. Wyatt was capable and responsible. Jeffrey was fine. He'd had a fantastic day, and now he was asleep. That was that.

"Hey," Cole said quietly. Andrea hadn't heard him come in, and she flinched. "How are you holding up?"

"I'm fine," Andrea said, but her shaky voice gave her away.

"Hmm." The low sound made Andrea think of a cello or a double bass. Cole dug through the drawer of the reception desk and pulled out a small bottle that glinted poison-green in the light coming through the wide front windows.

"Is that absinthe?" A glimmer of humor slinked through Andrea's overwrought nerves, and her lips twitched up in a tentative smile.

"Starla thinks she's hiding it from me," he said wryly. "I check it every now and then, and she's never actually opened it."

"Saving it for a special occasion?"

"Does an emergency qualify?" Cole didn't wait for an answer. He crossed the room, bottle in hand, and sat beside Andrea on one of the worn chairs. "I'm confiscating it. Want some?"

Andrea accepted the bottle and took the first sip. Sweet anise burned a trail down her throat, and she hissed as she handed it back to Cole.

"That'll wake you up in the morning."

"Maybe it grows on you," he said with a shrug and a swig.

"Thanks." Andrea's fingers brushed Cole's as he handed the bottle back, and a zing of awareness rushed through her. She took another gulp of the absinthe and asked, "How long has she worked here? You two seem close."

"A year or so." Cole paused, thinking. "Closer to two."

"But you've known her longer than that?"

"We're from the same neighborhood," he confirmed. "I used to see her around when I went back to visit family. Saw her grow up, fall in with a bad crowd."

"How did she end up here?" Andrea asked.

"She was living with a guy who didn't treat her right. No surprise. One of those kids who grew up in a family that treated her the same way. Just got used to it, you know? Anyway, when she'd finally had enough of it, I offered her a job here. Helped her find an apartment nearby and fix up a used car."

"That was... incredibly kind of you."

Cole shrugged, looking straight ahead. "I needed a receptionist."

"And she was the best person for the job?" Andrea asked dryly.

He glanced at her, a hint of a grin lighting his dark eyes,

and took another sip of absinthe. "I had to sink some time into training her," he admitted. "But yeah, she's a solid worker now."

"She has a crush on you." A slight edge of warning crept into Andrea's tone.

"Better me than a guy who would take advantage of that fact." Cole offered Andrea the absinthe. She shook her head, so he screwed the lid back on.

"So the feeling isn't mutual?"

"Might not be against the law, but she's basically young enough to be my daughter," Cole scoffed, sounding offended. Or something else... more like he was genuinely repulsed by the idea of it. "It's just puppy love. She'll find a guy her own age when she's ready. Until then, she's safe here."

"Like girls who fall for movie stars."

He looked straight at her and raised one eyebrow. "Are you comparing me to George Clooney?"

"No." Andrea laughed and hoped that the dim light hid her blush. "I just meant that girls who aren't ready for a real relationship tend to fall for men who are untouchable. It's safer."

That got another noncommittal grunt from Cole, and they were quiet for a minute.

"You must be hungry. We never did get to eat that pie for supper," he said. She didn't have much of an appetite, but she kept quiet as he stood and walked over to the vending machine in the corner. He considered the offerings for a moment before pulling some coins from his pocket and punching in the number, then returned with a packet of peanut butter sandwich crackers.

"Thanks." Andrea accepted the plastic package, touched

by the gesture. Cole sat down next to her again, though there were other chairs available, and Andrea offered him the first of the square sandwich crackers. He took it, and Andrea bit into the second one, more to give the absinthe in her stomach something to chew on than out of hunger.

In the absence of conversation, intrusive thoughts crept back into Andrea's mind. Thoughts of blood and bereaved mothers, of icy wind and Jeffrey's ordeal in the mountains. She checked her phone, but there was still no reply from Wyatt. Suddenly she missed her father so much that it felt like a hole in her chest. Cole sat beside her silently, ready to listen or to sit without talking for as long as she needed, and that loosened something in Andrea's chest.

"My dad died recently. He was on a camping trip with my son." She didn't even make a conscious decision to start talking, but suddenly she was. Talking on and on about how her dad used to take her son on these amazing trips, how he would draw up a detailed itinerary and always be back in time so that she and her mother wouldn't worry. Until one day he didn't. She told Cole about Jeffrey's misadventures off trail and the father-son team who had rescued him, how her dad never came back, how that bereavement all tied together with her son's salvation had left her not knowing which way was up. And at some point in all the talking, tears started coursing down her cheeks and wouldn't stop.

Cole put an arm around her, and Andrea buried her face in his shoulder, feeling grateful and embarrassed all at once.

"You must think I'm a total wacko." Andrea chuckled through her tears. "In the few days that you've known me, I've griped at you, insulted you, baked you a pie, invited myself to your house, accused you of kidnapping—God, when I say it out loud, I sound like a crazy person."

"I know what it's like to lose someone you love," Cole said softly. "I don't think you're crazy."

Andrea pulled back slightly to look up at him, but he was looking off into the middle distance, his expression closed. She wasn't going to repay his patience by digging into the most painful parts of his past. Instead, she shrugged his arm off and dug into her purse for a tissue to blow her nose. Her phone lit up, and her heart sped as she opened a text from Wyatt.

Sorry, just saw this. We were watching a movie. Jeff's great! Finally fell asleep in the epic blanket fort we set up in the living room. Gonna go to sleep too. Will call in the morning.

Andrea breathed a sigh of relief. She was surprised to see how late it was. Pushing herself to her feet, she said to Cole, "I should get going. I've taken up enough of your time. Thank you for not tossing me out. And for being so kind in spite of... well, you know." She shrugged sheepishly.

"No worries. Most of my dinners look like this," Cole said, holding up the empty package of peanut butter crackers, "so I'll take an accusation in exchange for fresh apple pie."

"I owe you a home-cooked meal," Andrea said before she could change her mind. "Would you come to my house for dinner? Say the day after tomorrow?"

It took him a moment to reply, and she was half sure that he'd refuse. Then his face twitched into one of his almost smiles, and he said, "How can I say no to good food?" He stood, and Andrea's heart hammered in her chest. "What time?"

She swallowed nervously. "Six?"

"Works for me. I'll walk you out."

It was freezing outside, but the fresh air cleared Andrea's head. Instantly, she felt steadier.

"Drive safe," Cole said as Andrea climbed into her car.

"Thanks."

She sat there for a minute after he had closed her door, watching him walk away. It was hard to trust her feelings when her nerves were so on edge, but she felt warm inside in a way that she hadn't in a long time... and it wasn't entirely due to the absinthe.

She was starting to understand why Starla had a crush on Cranky Cole.

12

FALLYN

"Sounds horrible," Molly said. "That poor girl..."

Fallyn had just finished filling her friend in on the events of the night before. "They haven't released anything about the blood, but given the situation, the stolen plates and all that, I feel pretty certain that the sock belonged to Wren."

"So what are you thinking? If you can share, I mean."

"Nothing is really gelling for me yet. Quite a few people with a motive against Graham. He's a polarizing figure, for sure. We've been doing a lot of poking around into his enemies. He provided a list of people who he felt could potentially look to do him harm." She pulled her phone away from her ear for a brief moment, tapped the screen, then sighed, "And that list is about to include me if he doesn't respond to my calls soon. You'd think it'd be a huge priority, but the best I've gotten is his secretary. I guess he was at some kind of photoshoot, and he's been doing lots of press today to get the word out, but still..."

"Well, I hope he gets back to you soon. Did the police not bring him the news about the sock and all?"

"I'm guessing they're waiting to confirm that it was definitely Wren's before getting them all panicked," Fallyn said, fiddling with her pen as she looked down at the three photographs sitting on the open manila folder on the desk in front of her. "The mechanic had security footage from the night he loaned out the car and the day it was returned. It's grainy, but they've got the guy on camera. Hopefully once they enhance it and get it out there circulating, it will turn something up."

"It sounds like things are progressing, at least. More and more evidence is coming out, which can only be a good thing."

It *did* sound that way, but Fallyn couldn't quite make herself feel it. "Somehow it still doesn't seem like we're anywhere close to solving it." A rush of irritation hit her as she said the words, and she shoved the thought from her mind momentarily. "How about you, though, Molly? Things still going well?" She hadn't seen the woman since their last Sunday dinner a couple of weeks before.

"We have two couples staying with us right now at the B and B," the older woman said. "They're lovely. I'm actually throwing their lunch together right now. And with Griff, everything is *wonderful*."

The woman's voice changed subtly when she talked about him, and it warmed Fallyn's anxious heart for a brief moment to hear it. "I'm happy to hear it. I'm hoping to solve this case and get back for our next Sunday dinner since we had to miss today."

"I'll make sure it's extra special for when you come back. But don't let me keep you from your work any longer. It was good talking to you."

"See you soon," Fallyn said.

The woman responded in kind, and Fallyn felt another burst of impatience as she hung up and looked at her empty notifications. Should she try to set something up with Alicia for now and just wait?

"How was Molly?" David asked, looking up from his computer.

"She was good," Fallyn said, then grabbed the keys off the table and made a beeline for her jacket. "But I'm tired of waiting on Graham to answer his phone. What do you say we go pay him a visit?"

David rapped on the door, and the same housekeeper from the previous day let it swing open a few seconds later. This time, though, he didn't simply stand aside and beckon them in. "I assume you have business with Representative Hazelton, but you'll have to make an appointment if you want to speak with him. He's very busy and-"

"We really need to speak with him," Shaw said firmly. "There's been an important development in his daughter's case."

They'd agreed they wouldn't mention the sock or the blood, but she was very interested in seeing if he had any reaction to a picture of the man in the loaner Subaru.

The housekeeper's gaze strayed to the manila folder Fallyn had clutched in front of her, and he went silent for a long moment. His expression turned to one of resignation, though, and he said, "Is it time-sensitive? His schedule is very full today, and he just got back from an event where he was speaking about his daughter."

"It is."

To Fallyn's relief, a moment later, they were led inside.

When they got to Graham's office door, the housekeeper tapped at it twice, then opened it.

"Mr. Shaw and Ms. Rappaport here to see you, sir. They claim it's important."

Hazelton's expression was one Fallyn could only describe as bewildered, and his normally neat hair stuck out in tufts, as if he'd been tugging at it. Still, the slick smile came readily.

"Hello there," he said, dismissing their guide with a curt nod. "I was going to get back to you shortly, but I've been a bit busy, sorry. What can I do for you?" He gestured for them to sit.

Fallyn took her seat, pulling out the manila folder. "There were a few developments late last night, and I wanted to get your reaction to it all."

"Alright," he said, rubbing at his temples with one hand and clenching the other into a fist.

"The police are looking for a person of interest who borrowed a loaner from a local mechanic shop. I picked out a few stills for you to look at."

His eyes went wide, and his hand darted out for the folder as she slid it toward him. He flipped through the images quickly and shook his head.

"No, sorry, I—I don't recognize him."

Fallyn nodded, disappointment surging through her. "Are you sure? It's not super clear, but maybe it's ringing some faint bell."

Graham stared at the picture a short while longer, then

shook his head. Before he could speak, though, the door swung open, and his secretary walked in.

"Mr. Hazelton, I need to speak with you for a moment...alone?"

Fallyn turned around to see a pale, nervous ghost of the woman she'd met the day before.

"Can it wait?" Graham said. "We're in the middle of something. If you could just give me five or ten more minutes, I—"

"It can't wait, sir."

Graham stood, moving quickly toward the door. He turned to Fallyn and Shaw. "Sorry about this. I'll be right back."

"I wonder what's going on?" Fallyn whispered once the door swung shut behind them.

David shrugged. "Who knows?"

She was about to hazard a few guesses, but her gaze locked on to Graham Hazelton's hulking, mahogany desk—specifically on a slip of paper half sticking out from beneath a black covered book titled *Daily Planner*. She could only make out a few words of the hand-printed note, but what she did see had her palms going damp.

She elbowed Shaw hard in the shoulder and jerked her chin toward the desk.

"Do you see what I see?"

Shaw leaned in and let out a low gasp.

"Holy cow."

You have until Tuesday evening to secure one million dollars cash if –

The rest of the words were obscured, but Fallyn wasn't

about to let that stop her. She rose and bent over the desk, tugging the note from behind the planner.

You have until Tuesday evening to secure one million dollars cash if you want your daughter back unharmed. At that time, I will contact you to set up a drop off spot for the money. Once I ensure it's unmarked and get clear of the area, I will send you a location where you can pick Wren up safely the following evening.

TELL NO ONE. I'm watching you. No cops. No funny business, or you won't like what happens next.

Taped to the bottom of the note? A tiny snapshot of Wren dressed in the same nightclothes she'd been taken in, newspaper in hand. On the cover? The little girl's face with a MISSING headline.

Wren was alive.

Right as Fallyn snapped an image of the note on her phone, low voices sounded from the hallway just outside the door. Fallyn quickly tucked the piece of paper back in its place and dropped to her seat seconds before the door swung open again.

Graham stepped in, white as a sheet.

"Everything okay?" she asked, heart hammering from both the close call and the expression on the man's face.

"Apparently, there was blood in the car at that mechanic's shop." He shook his head, rubbing at his temples. "Dear God, up until now, I had this...I don't know, gut feeling that she was safe. And now I'm not so sure."

Fallyn nodded slowly, trying not to show her hand. "Was that the police? Did they say if the blood belonged to Wren?"

He sat heavily in his chair and leaned forward to press his head into his hand.

"No. No, it was a close contact who has a friend on the force. They haven't determined who the blood belonged to yet."

"Okay, that's good news then. Maybe she is still unharmed."

It took everything she had not to let her gaze flicker back to the spot where the note was hidden.

Why was he so terrified when the kidnapper had not only assured him of Wren's safety in the ransom letter but had sent a picture? Seemed to her like Graham would feel relieved that his daughter was still alive. Instead, he seemed more scared than she'd seen him to date.

So strange.

She put that thought aside to chew on for later and then turned to Shaw.

"We should probably give Graham some time to process all this." She turned to face the Congressman. "Thanks for your time. We'll be in touch."

The two of them remained silent until they got into the car and closed the door behind them.

"Holy crap," she said, shaking her head in shock. "So now what?"

Shaw stared back at her, wide-eyed. "Hell if I know. We can't go to the police. If they decide to make a move and the kidnapper is truly watching Graham, that could spell catastrophe for Wren."

It was a risk neither of them was willing to take.

"Hazelton has the money. I'm sure he'll do whatever it takes to free up those funds and pay it," she reasoned.

"So are you saying we just wait and let it unfold?"

That seemed like a risk in itself. Especially with someone like Graham Hazelton at the helm.

"I honestly don't know. I hate the idea of Alicia not knowing her baby girl is still alive. But at least she *is*, you know? And we have reasonable assurance she'll stay that way for the next couple of days. Let's lay low and think this through in the meantime. One misstep and..."

She couldn't finish that thought. Her stomach swirled as she and David began driving back to the bed and breakfast.

On one hand, the case had just taken a massive turn for the better. There was a very good chance that Wren was currently very much alive and well and that she could stay that way. But there was still something that niggled at Fallyn about it all...

Something that felt wrong.

What were they missing?

13

BOBBIE

"Okay, thanks." Marcus disconnected a call as Bobbie climbed back into the car and turned to face her. "That was the detective we spoke to yesterday. Wren Hazelton's mother approved the reward, so we're all set."

"Excellent. So the operation is a go," Bobbie said, managing a smile. Then she slumped back in her seat without starting the car. It was a small win in the scheme of things, and until Wren was found, it wasn't much to celebrate about. "Every time I think about it, I feel sick to my stomach. That little girl must be so scared."

"It's terrible," Marcus agreed. He brought one of Bobbie's hands up to his mouth and kissed her knuckles. They sat there in solemn silence until Archie let out a squall of protest. Bobbie reclaimed her hand and started up the car.

"Okay, okay, we're going!"

Marcus reached back and handed Archie one of his frozen teethers as the car warmed up. They made quick work of the special mini editions of the *Bee* she'd printed up, taking turns running them into stores and restaurants or staying in the car with Archie. His patience had worn thin by their last stop, so Marcus freed Archie from his car seat and pulled a cozy hat down over his ears. They grinned at each other—so different and yet exactly the same, like looking into a funhouse mirror—and Bobbie's heart felt like it might fly right out of her chest.

"What?" Marcus grinned across the hood of the car at Bobbie, and she realized that she had been staring. Her usual defense mechanisms sparked, and she almost shrugged him off and turned away. Instead, she looked him in the eye and told him the truth.

"You two are so beautiful together, it makes my heart ache."

Marcus circled around the car to kiss her. "Right back at you. Come on, let's get some food."

They walked around to the front of the building, and Bobbie froze on the sidewalk. This bagel shop was where Mildred Taylor had spilled the beans about Archie. It was where Marcus had learned about his son... and about Bobbie's betrayal. Tears stung her eyes as she clutched the reward fliers to her chest, just more proof that Marcus was an amazing, selfless human being. How could he forgive her for what she'd done, truly? How long before the novelty of family life wore off and resentment took over?

How long before he ran away, like everyone else?

"Bobbie?" Marcus doubled back and put an arm around her. "Are you okay?"

She just pressed her face into his shoulder and swallowed back her tears. Archie's little hand patted her knit cap.

"It was a bad few minutes," Marcus said softly. "It was

also the best day of my life, even if it didn't feel like it at the time. We're okay."

Bobbie lifted her face up and kissed him, still blinking back tears. Marcus wasn't a runner. He never had been. *She* was the one who had run away, and she wasn't going to do that again. Bobbie was done running. She was putting down roots here, together with her little family.

She nodded up at Marcus, and they walked into the bagel shop hand in hand. Marcus stood in line surveying the long list of bagels and spreads while Bobbie set their special edition of the *Bee* on top of the few copies that remained of her latest issue. She went back to stand next to Marcus and planted a big kiss on Archie's chubby cheek. Marcus may have missed the months that their son had looked like a little old man, but he had still come onto the scene early in Archie's life, all things considered. He'd been there for his first Thanksgiving, would be there for his first Christmas, and there were so many more firsts still ahead of them.

"There's my little muffin!" Mildred squealed, rushing out of the back office. Archie matched her energy, talking to her in a stream of baby babble and launching himself into her outstretched arms. "Aren't you just the cutest little pumpkin? Yes you are!"

"Hi, Mildred," Bobbie said when the woman paused her baby talk long enough to glance between Archie's parents. "This is Marcus. He's Archie's dad."

Shock followed by the elation of juicy gossip flashed across Mildred's face, but her reaction time was mercifully short.

"Pleased to meet you, Marcus. I see where Archie gets his good looks!"

"Thank you," Marcus said politely before stepping up to the counter to order. Mildred stepped aside, still bouncing Archie on her hip. As the TV mounted above her office door segued into its next segment, Mildred eyed the screen with a frown.

"Did you see this?" she asked Bobbie.

"See what?"

"They've released a composite drawing and video of a person of interest in the Wren Hazelton case."

What she could see wasn't all that encouraging. The face was largely hidden. He had a straight, unremarkable nose, lean cheeks, and firm mouth. The description beneath it pegged him at around six feet tall, average build. A moment later, a video clip played. Despite the attempts to zoom in close, it was grainy and about as helpful as the drawing.

"I guess if that was a friend or something, I might be able to pick him out, but I don't think I'd recognize him if he walked in right now," Mildred murmured, echoing Bobbie's thoughts.

The Cherry Blossom Point police phone number scrolled across the bottom for a moment before Graham Hazelton's face filled the screen. His wife wasn't by his side this morning, just Graham in front of a podium, looking as polished and put together as always. The TV was muted, but the text on the bottom of the screen said that he was offering an award of fifty thousand dollars for any information about his missing daughter.

"Interesting timing," Mildred said. "You and your sweetheart do this nice thing and *now* Daddy Warbucks comes in with the cash? Just strange he didn't do that from the start, don't you think?"

"It's strange," Bobbie admitted. Then she shrugged. "But I can't imagine that degree of stress. I know that I wouldn't be able to think straight if I didn't know where my baby was or if he was safe."

"True enough. I shouldn't judge."

"If Marcus inspired Hazelton to put up an even bigger reward, well... that's a good thing, right?" Bobbie looked back up at the TV as the news cut to a reporter standing outside of some government building. The number of a tip line appeared at the bottom of the screen.

"I suppose it is. I just pray that little girl gets home safe."

"And soon." Bobbie turned and held her hands out for Archie. Mildred relinquished him with a parting bit of baby talk and headed back into her office, and Bobbie walked back over to Marcus.

"I got lunch and dessert," he announced happily. "One basil bagel with sundried tomato cream cheese, and a blueberry bagel with strawberry cream cheese. Split them with me?"

"That sounds fantastic." Bobbie hugged him with her baby-free arm, suddenly overwhelmed with gratitude that her little family was together and safe. "Thank you."

When they got back to the house, she tried to focus on the fact that things had taken a positive turn. There was more information than ever coming out, and she tried to allow herself to be comforted by the idea that they had done *something* about this atrocity that had happened in their safe little town. Even if the only thing they had accomplished was spurring the little girl's father to act... well, that wasn't nothing.

Bobbie rescued a now-irate Archie from the restraints of

his car seat and smooshed a hat down over his ears before carrying him from the car to the house. It was only autumn, but the chill wind today packed a punch. Marcus carried Archie's diaper bag over from the car, but he dropped it inside the door without going in. Bobbie shot him a questioning look.

"What's up?"

"I'm sure you have work to catch up on for next month's big holiday edition," Marcus told her, smiling apologetically, "and I have some stuff to do myself, so I'll be back for dinner time if that's okay. I can take this little fellow with me on my errands, though."

"No, it's okay." Bobbie smiled through a sudden vertigo and held her baby closer. "He's overdue for a nap."

"Yeah, okay." Marcus was still smiling, more or less, but there was a strange edge to his expression that made Bobbie's stomach do an unpleasant little flip.

"Is everything okay?" she asked. "Are we okay?"

"Always." Marcus kissed Archie's cheek. "I'll see you later, little man. Have a good sleep."

Archie waved his father off and made his goodbye noise, which was more or less a B sound on repeat. Bobbie pulled one side of her oversized winter coat over her son as they stood and watched his father drive away.

Something was off. Although Marcus still had his own place, he spent nearly all of his time with Bobbie and their son. Going off all of a sudden with only a vague mention of errands was completely out of character. What was that about?

Archie started to fuss, and Bobbie carried him into the warmth of their house. She changed his diaper and nursed him to sleep, comforted by their daily rhythm. But as soon as Archie nodded off, her worries roared back onto center stage.

Was it going back to the bagel shop that had thrown Marcus for a loop? That was where he had found out about Archie... and he could try and reassure her all he wanted, but Bobbie knew how hard that news had hit him. To learn in public and from a stranger that Bobbie had been hiding their child from him for so long, that she hadn't told him the truth even when she saw him in person... God, how could he even *pretend* to be over that? How could he forgive her when she couldn't even forgive herself?

No wonder he wanted some time away from her.

Bobbie shoved the thought away and threw herself into her work. If she couldn't shake this restless feeling, she could at least put the energy buzzing through her to good use. Her December issue was all wrapped up, but she was behind schedule on January. The looming holidays felt so all-encompassing that it was hard to see past them, and she still needed to outline the next issue. What would keep people's attention in the new year?

Bobbie sifted through her long list of ideas for articles, and the one about the best spots to sled around town hit her in the gut. That had been such a perfect day with Marcus. The memory of it must be charred to ash for him now, knowing that they were out laughing on the slopes when all the while his *son* was there in town, with him none the wiser. Bobbie growled in frustration and tried to focus on her work, but her eyes kept glazing over.

She couldn't stop thinking about that weird little exchange on her front step.

Where *was* he?

Bobbie shut her laptop with a sigh of defeat. Her brain wasn't going to cooperate with anything work-related right now. Well, she had a bit of time to herself for once. It was the perfect opportunity to wrap Christmas gifts.

Her mood lifted slightly as she went through all of the hiding spots in her little house, uncovering the presents that she had collected for Archie and his daddy. Most of her gifts for Marcus had pictures of Archie printed on them; she had gone a bit gaga on the design-your-own-gift sites. But there were some other things too, like a heavy wool sweater that Marcus would need for his first winter in Maine.

...if he stayed.

Swatting away intrusive thoughts like that one all the while, Bobbie wrapped up the gifts. Nearly all of Archie's gifts were things that she and Marcus had picked out together, browsing online stores long after their baby had fallen asleep. It was just a matter of transferring them from the cardboard boxes they'd come in to shiny wrapping paper that Archie would have a blast ripping to bits.

Bobbie needed something to mark the gifts as being for *Daddy* or for *Archie*, and the mechanical pencils that she used for work weren't going to cut it. She went rummaging through their junk drawer for something more substantial—but then a scribbled list in Marcus's handwriting caught her eye.

call plumber
gifts for mom and dad
oil change
clean out car
call devlin re: feb

Bobbie froze. Devlin was Marcus's supervisor, the one

who organized the group of doctors working in Mozambique. Was Marcus heading back to Africa in *February*? That was so soon. What about Archie's first birthday? His first steps? Marcus had been gutted to learn that he had missed so many little milestones already. Bobbie had been certain that he planned to stick around for the big ones.

But they had never actually had that conversation. This was his life's work, his calling. Did she really think he'd stick around for her? No, she had never been able to convince herself of that. But for *Archie*? She had really thought that Marcus would stay.

The words of the note blurred in front of Bobbie's eyes, and she crumpled to the floor. He was leaving. He was running away, just like everyone else. Just like she had always known he would, try as she might to believe otherwise. He'd had their fill of them, and he had no intention of spending a full winter in Maine. Of course not. Why would he?

But... Archie. How could he possibly...?

Just a couple of minutes after the waterworks had started, Bobbie dried her tears and picked herself up off the cold floor. This had always been the plan. She had been ready and willing to raise Archie alone. And whatever Marcus did, she wasn't *alone* alone anymore. She knew that he would insist on supporting his son, that he would want to spend as much time with him as possible when he was stateside. And Bobbie would have to be content with that. She certainly wasn't in a position to make demands. And she really, truly didn't want Marcus to grow to resent her for taking him away from his dream job.

A few tissues later, Bobbie marked the presents with a shaking hand and put everything away.

Everything was going to be fine. They would make the best of it. They could FaceTime daily. Marcus going away for work was something they could handle.

So why didn't he tell you about it? asked that horrible little voice in the back of her mind.

That was the scariest part. If they were a real family living together in one house, he would have consulted her. They would have figured it out together.

But he hadn't even mentioned it. She didn't factor in.

Bobbie hid the Christmas gifts away, feeling a whole lot worse than she had when she'd taken them out of hiding an hour before. Whatever happened, she had her perfect baby. She and Archie would just have to make the best of things.

No matter how low her mood got, there was one last stubborn ember of hope that refused to die. They were a family. That meant something. It meant something to *Marcus*. She knew it did.

She just hoped that her dream wasn't ending before it had even truly begun.

14

LENA

LENA STRETCHED out like a cat and then curled back into her duvet, feeling deliciously well-rested. It was early morning, Owen was already up, and Lena sprawled starfish-style for a minute before turning over to check on the baby. Addy was sound asleep in the side-car crib that Owen had attached to their bed to reduce the time they spent pacing the hallway at night, and a glance at the clock revealed that their baby had slept for over eight hours in a row—easily the longest stretch since they had brought her home.

The early-morning silence was blissful, and Lena just lay there admiring Addy's increasingly chubby cheeks and the peaceful rhythm of her breath. The homey smell of cooking bacon and the clatter of plastic toys told her that the other half of their household was already up and at it, but Lena was in no hurry to start her day. Between her small business and the two small humans that she and Owen had welcomed into their home, life had been incredibly hectic lately. Busyness and worry had a way of shouldering gratitude aside, even when she had so much to be grateful for. In rare moments like this one, Lena was able to sink into the full-body gratitude that her incredibly beautiful life deserved.

Addy blinked herself awake and took in some extra air with an Instagram-worthy yawn. Her face crumpled into a frown when she looked through the bars of her crib and saw an open door. Then she turned her head and saw Lena next to her, and her worry melted into a smile of recognition. Addy reached for her, and Lena sat up and scooped the baby into her arms.

As her baby girl snuggled into her, resting her whole body against Lena's and laying her head on Lena's shoulder, she felt a powerful rush of gratitude for her soft, round body. For so many years, she had felt uncomfortable in her own skin, had wished that she looked a bit more like the starved and edited women on the covers of magazines. And for what? The love of her life thought that she was perfect just as she was, and the soft lines of her body provided a safe and comforting landscape for this baby, who had so needed a soft place to land. In all her years, Lena had never felt so perfectly at home in her own body. She was exactly where she needed to be.

A dirty diaper spurred Lena out of her reverie and into action. She put a dry diaper on Addy and then slipped the baby's cozy jammies back on to take her downstairs. Sam lit up when he saw them, though of course his eyes were on Addy rather than Lena. But she was too full of contentment to let that bother her today. She was just happy to see him smile.

"Good morning!" Sam said to his baby sister, who responded with happy baby babble.

"That tower is taller than you!" Lena said, impressed. Sam gave her a quick, shy grin and looked away.

Gemma had dropped off a big box of Magna-tiles the day before, and Sam was using the jewel-toned plastic pieces to build all sorts of structures. The little boy had the mind of an engineer. There was so much going on in there. Sam went back to work, and Lena left him to it.

"There's my girls!" Owen said as Lena walked into the kitchen. He set down a full plate of bacon and pulled Lena in for a kiss, making Addy laugh. He dropped a noisy kiss on the baby's forehead and gave Lena a playful squeeze before going back to the stove.

"Thanks for letting me sleep in," Lena said.

"I wouldn't dream of interrupting your first full night of sleep in weeks. I slept well too, only been up for a half hour or so. Figured I'd get a jump start on breakfast. Sam requested bacon and waffles."

"A man after my own heart." Lena put Addy in her high chair and grabbed a jar of homemade baby food from the fridge. This one said *Sweet Potato and Liver* in Nikki's looping handwriting. Lena had been supremely skeptical of the combination, but Addy loved it.

Addy made a noise of protest at being stranded in her high chair with no food, and Lena handed the baby a wooden spoon to drum with while she warmed up her fortified sweet potato mush.

"Sammy boy!" Owen shouted as he plated up the first round of waffles. "Breakfast is ready!"

Sam came running into the kitchen and hopped onto a stool at the kitchen counter. He'd brought a stack of Magna-tiles, and he built a quick tower for Addy to smash while

Owen poured maple syrup over his blueberry-studded waffles.

"Thanks!" Sam said. Lately, Lena had noticed, Sam didn't call either of them by name. It was like he was stuck somewhere between Owen and Dad, reluctant to use either one. It was a kind of progress, she supposed. Or maybe she was just fabricating progress out of thin air. She turned her focus back to Addy, who was whining and reaching for the Magna-tiles that were now scattered across the kitchen floor.

Owen put a plate of food in front of Lena, and she managed to eat most of it in between spooning bites of sweet potato into Addy's wide-open mouth. Sam just about inhaled two rounds of waffles before running upstairs to get ready for school.

"Is Addy's bag ready for daycare?" Owen asked. They had started taking Addy to a daycare near Owen's studio for a few hours on weekday mornings so that Lena could catch up on work. The woman who ran it was an old high school friend of Gemma's, and she had started bringing baby Cara there the same week. That made it easier for Lena to hand Addy off, but it was still hard. After missing the first six months of Addy's life, the thought of missing even one more milestone tore Lena up inside. But she wasn't willing to let her new business fade into oblivion. She had only been balancing the demands of motherhood with the rest of her life for a few weeks, and already it felt overwhelming. Luckily she had an amazing partner and supportive family to help her.

"Yeah, I packed the diaper bag last night. Still needs snacks, though. I can add some if you want to get her cleaned up and dressed."

"Sure thing." Owen lifted the sweet potato-covered baby out of her seat and took her straight to the kitchen sink for a quick cleanup.

Once Addy was all clean and bundled up, Lena went out into the living room to say goodbye to Sam. Compared to Addy, he often seemed big and grown-up. But just now, standing next to Owen and wearing a slightly oversized coat, he looked so young. Lena felt an overwhelming rush of affection for the little boy, and she stepped forward to give him a hug. But when she started to open her arms, he stiffened visibly and looked away. Lena settled for zipping up his coat and pulling his handmade cap onto his head.

"There. Ready for school."

"Got everything you need?" Owen asked him.

"Yep." Sam opened the door and ran for the car.

"And we're out of here." Holding Addy in one arm, Owen bent down for one last kiss. "Have a good morning, love."

"You too. I'll pick Addy up today."

"Sounds good. I'll get Sam from school."

"Spaghetti and salad for dinner?" Lena wasn't much of a cook, but she had been trying to make more home-cooked meals for Sam—and even she could handle spaghetti and salad.

"Perfect." Owen grabbed Addy's bag and headed out. Lena stood out front, relishing the cold morning air as she watched her family drive off. Before she had even turned to go back inside, Gemma pulled into the driveway.

"Great timing," Lena said as she greeted her with a hug. "How was drop-off?"

"Super smooth today."

"Awesome."

"Oh, wait!" Gemma spun around and ran back to her car. "Almost forgot!" She tossed Lena a package of dry-erase markers and then pulled a huge whiteboard out of the back of her car.

"Nice," Lena said, half laughing. Gemma had been a huge help to her ever since Lena had brought her on board, but her passion and professionalism lately had been next-level. Between putting Cara in daycare and sharing the daily work of parenting with Patrick, Gemma was a new woman. Her grief and exhaustion had faded away, and she was more like the bubbly girl Lena remembered than she had been in a long time.

With Gemma's help, Lena managed to get a full day's work done before lunch. As they cleaned up their mess and turned their office back into a dining table, Lena's mind shifted back into parenting mode.

"Hey, Gem," she ventured, "can I ask your advice on something?"

"Always."

"Thanks." Lena glanced at the time and saw that they still had nearly an hour before daycare pickup. "Come through to the kitchen, and I'll see what I can pull together for lunch."

"You're a lifesaver. The kids are doing school lunches this month, and I completely forgot to pack myself something."

"We've always got enough food. Maybe not, you know, a meal. But food." Lena rummaged through the fridge and started pulling out the basic components of a good snack platter. Three types of cheese, cured meats, some crunchy veggies... She set them on the counter next to the crackers Gemma had found and started slicing.

"What did you want to ask about?" Gemma grabbed a second cutting board and knife and worked on cutting a bell pepper into strips.

"Sam," Lena said on an exhale. "He barely looks at me. I don't want to push him too hard or overwhelm him or anything, but I don't want to just ignore him for Addy either. I just don't know how to connect with him. He's not open to it."

Gemma was quiet for a while, thinking. Then she said, "Zoe opens up to me the most when we're busy with something else, working together just the two of us. She loves baking and crafts, but it could be anything Sam's into."

"One-on-one time," Lena said thoughtfully.

"Totally. Even driving in the car together works. That's when my boys talk to me the most, when we're driving somewhere. Something about looking at the same thing instead of looking at each other makes talking easier, I think."

"Thanks, Gem. I'll see what I can think up."

"It'll get easier."

Lena nodded and smiled, but it felt forced. She had trouble believing that things would get easier between her and Sam, but she deeply hoped that they would. More than anything, she wanted Sam and Addy to feel safe and cherished. It was hard to accept that she couldn't make anyone feel anything. All she could do was create a warm, stable environment and hope that Sam came around. He had been through so much. More than anything, she needed to be steady and patient. He had to see that they would be there for him no matter what.

Just as they sat down to enjoy their snack-platter lunch, there was a knock on the door.

"Hello hello!" a man called, not waiting for an answer before opening the door and stepping into her house. Gemma looked toward the living room with a startled frown, but Lena just shook her head and laughed. She knew that voice.

"Freddy?" she called, hopping off her kitchen stool and walking into the next room.

"There you are!" Freddy stood in the center of her living room, dressed in an emerald-green suit and a ridiculous fur hat. "And more or less intact despite a sudden initiation to motherhood. You don't look terrible."

"Thanks," Lena said dryly. She accepted a hug from Freddy that offered a bare minimum of human contact. "What are you doing here?"

"Gayle invited me to your shower, but I was in Monaco. I didn't even see the invitation until I got home. I've been through five assistants since you quit. No one compares, and as a result, my life is in shambles." He sighed dramatically. "Anyway, I've brought you an elephant."

"A what?!" Lena ran to the window. Behind her, Gemma burst out laughing. Sure enough, there were two men on her front walk laboriously hauling a life-sized baby elephant stuffie toward her house. The thing had a saddle on its back that was big enough for Sam.

"A baby shower gift," Freddy drawled. He looked at her with something approaching concern, as if worried that motherhood had lowered her IQ.

Lena laughed, charmed in spite of herself. "That was very... thoughtful."

"I wanted to get you something you wouldn't already have."

"Mission accomplished."

They helped the men steer the huge stuffie through Lena's mercifully oversized front door and carried it through to the playroom. Freddy looked around the large space, wrinkling his nose at the piles of toys and the paint-smeared craft table.

"I've got to go," Gemma said with a chuckle. "I have a couple of errands to run on my way to pick Cara up. Enjoy your elephant."

"Thanks, Gem. See you later. Take some food!" Lena called after her.

"Didn't this room used to be your own personal gallery?" Freddy asked.

Lena grinned, surprised that he remembered anything about her house. "Yeah, it did. I've evolved."

Freddy made a noncommittal sound. "You've certainly changed."

"People do that."

"Not that I've noticed." Freddie lifted one foot and brushed a stray bit of Play-Doh off his shiny leather shoe. He walked back into the living room and picked up a large gift bag that Lena hadn't noticed in the commotion.

"*More* presents?"

"A few odds and ends." He waved one hand dismissively and went to study a new watercolor painting that hung on her living room wall. Lena sat on her couch and dug into the gift bag. The loot included a tiny cashmere sweater, an original copy of The Wizard of Oz, a sterling silver rattle, and...

"Is this an iPad?" Lena demanded.

Freddy turned to her and raised his eyebrows. "For the boy. For... games? School? Whatever it is that they do," he said, waving a flippant hand.

"This is all... incredibly generous. Thank you."

He shrugged and looked around. "Where are the children?"

"School and daycare," Lena said.

Freddy made a hmm sound.

"Did you want to meet them?" she asked, touched. "You could stay a while, come with me to pick Addy up."

"Maybe some other time. I should get back to the grind."

"What are you working on right now?"

"*Elves on Strike.*" Freddy tucked his fur hat under one arm and tossed his platinum hair. "I'm assembling it in place in a gallery in Portland. Very cutting edge."

"What happened to focusing on painting?"

"I've been focusing on painting, darling. But if I don't do something else on occasion, I'll die of boredom. Once this is done, be it a smash success or a stunning failure, I can go back into hiding and enjoy my solitude for a while. Create a few more masterpieces."

"That sounds... reasonable."

"I'm always reasonable."

Lena covered a laugh up with a cough. Freddy walked toward the door, and Lena stood to walk him out. As the truck pulled away, the seed of an idea germinated in Lena's mind.

"Hey Freddy, where did you get that truck?"

"I've got a hookup that I use for all my larger

installations...They've got flatbeds, standard tow trucks, you name it."

"Would you give me that number?" Lena asked.

Thanks to Freddy's completely impractical gift, suddenly she knew exactly how to create some quality one-on-one time with Sam...

15

ANDREA

THE TOMATOES in front of her faded into a jumbled mass of red, and she blinked her gritty eyes. Sleep had been hard to come by since the other night, and she had a feeling that was going to be the status quo until Wren Hazelton had been found.

"Hey, Mom?"

Andrea jerked up and forced a smile at Jeffrey, who stood on the opposite side of the kitchen table. The split lip he'd come home from school with was looking even worse. She had tried to convince him to ice it, but he had waved her off.

"Yeah, buddy?"

"Is this a date?"

Andrea fumbled the colander she held, and half a dozen of the cherry tomatoes went flying across the counter. She must have misheard him.

"What?"

"Is it a date?" he asked in the same neutral tone. "The guy who's coming over for dinner. The mechanic. You've been cooking since I got home."

Since before then, actually, but she wasn't about to admit to that.

"Definitely not. It's not a date," Andrea told him.

As if she would include her kid on a–

As if she and Cole would *ever*–

Her mind sputtered like an engine that wouldn't start.

"You can have a date, you know."

"I'm aware," Andrea said dryly.

"It's just been a really long time." Jeffrey stood with his arms crossed, giving her a worried look. "I'm not going to live here with you forever. It would be okay for you to have a boyfriend, like Wyatt's mom does."

Ah, she thought. *There it is.*

"You like him?" she asked. "Sadie's boyfriend?"

"Trent?" Jeffrey shrugged. "He seems cool. She smiles a lot when he's around. He makes her laugh."

"Well. That's nice. But Cole—that is, the mechanic—isn't a laughy kind of guy. And it's not a date."

"Okay."

"I'm just grateful to have a working car, and Cole said that he eats most of his meals out of a vending machine. So I figured I'd have him over for some real food."

She'd just leave out the part about how she invited herself over his house to snoop and all but accused him of kidnapping a little girl.

"That's sad."

"Yeah."

Jeffrey walked over to the fridge and pulled out a bottle of orange juice, which he proceeded to drink without bothering to grab a glass. Before Andrea could comment on that, he hissed in pain and pulled the bottle away from his mouth.

"Your lip?" she asked.

"Yeah." Jeffrey put the top back on the bottle and shoved it back into the fridge.

"You said you got that from a bike?"

He shook his head. "Tripped and hit my face on the bike rack."

That didn't sound like him, but she *had* seen bouts of clumsiness following growth spurts, like he was figuring out how to move through the world all over again. And he had probably grown three inches in as many months. Plus, he must have a million things on his mind after all that had happened. She just wished he would talk to *her* about some of them. Then again, she should just be grateful that he had Wyatt as a stand-in big brother who could help him acclimate to being in a new town.

"Are you done with your homework?" she asked, mostly just to keep herself from asking more prying questions about his day.

"Almost," Jeff said. He chugged a glass of water and then continued, "Everything but math."

"If you get that out of the way, we'll have time for a couple episodes of *Stranger Things* before bed."

"Cool." Jeffrey opened his math textbook on the kitchen table and got to work while Andrea finished throwing together a simple salad. The pot roast was out of the oven, and the rest of the sides would be done any minute. She had made green bean casserole, caramelized Brussels sprouts, roasted delicata squash, and Parmesan roasted potatoes. If this was going to be Cole's only proper dinner this week, she intended to make it a good one.

When the doorbell rang, Andrea's heart started racing again.

Not a date, she scolded herself as she dried her hands and went to answer the door. She couldn't believe that she had let her son's question get under her skin. Maybe she needed to show him that she could still laugh and smile, no boyfriend required. Or maybe he was missing his grandfather like crazy and needed more men in his life, not just the older brother figure he had in Wyatt. Or maybe–

Maybe she should shelve those maybes for another time.

Andrea opened the door and smiled up at Cole. Suddenly she felt acutely aware of everything around her: the fresh night air and the curls that fell around her eyes... the way that Cole's dark gray sweater pulled tight across his chest.

"Hi." In his low-gravel voice, the sound was barely more word than grunt. But he held up a bottle of red wine—a good one—and Andrea was charmed.

"Hello," she said, accepting the bottle. "Thank you. You didn't need to do that."

"Couldn't show up empty-handed," Cole said.

"You could have. It's supposed to be a thank you dinner." A strong draft blasted through the door, and Andrea stepped back. "Come on in out of the cold."

Cole stepped inside and shed his jacket. He hung it on a peg next to her winter coat, and Andrea closed the door behind him.

"You're our first house guest," she told him, nervously filling the silence as she led him through to the kitchen. "We just moved to town a couple days before Thanksgiving."

"Place looks good."

"Thank you. I work from home, so getting settled in has been a priority. This is my son, Jeffrey."

Jeff barely glanced up from his textbook. "Hi."

"Jeffrey, this is Cole."

"Nice to meet you," he muttered, glaring down at the page.

"Are you almost done?" she asked.

"No. These word problems are impossible. They don't make any sense."

Cole sat down next to him and studied the textbook for a moment. Jeffrey gave him the side eye, his frown intensifying.

"What seems to be the trouble?" Cole asked.

Jeffrey prodded at a particular problem in response, and Cole nodded thoughtfully. His dark hair was slightly overgrown, curling over the backs of his ears. Andrea realized that she was staring and hurried across the kitchen to cut into the pot roast she had made. When she glanced over her shoulder, she saw Cole pick a spare pencil up off the table and jot an equation down.

"Try that."

Jeffrey's pencil scratched across the paper as he ran through the problem, and then he checked his answer in the back of the book. "We got it!"

"Can you figure out the next one?" Cole asked.

"I think so." Jeffrey bent over his work, reenergized.

Cole looked up at Andrea with something approaching a smile on his face. "Need any help?"

"Everything's ready. I just need to serve it up and set the table. Jeffrey?" That was usually his job.

"He's working," Cole grunted. "I can help."

He didn't flounder around helplessly like most guests would have, and he didn't ask where everything was. He just moved quickly and methodically through drawers and cabinets until he found what he needed. There was something extremely attractive about that casual competence.

"Done!" Jeffrey said triumphantly as Andrea set a loaded plate down by his elbow. He closed the textbook with a thump and pulled the plate in front of him.

"Cider?" Andrea asked. She opened the crockpot where fresh cider had been stewing all day with cinnamon sticks, star anise, orange zest, and a handful of cranberries. The steam that rose up when she lifted the lid smelled absurdly delicious.

"Yes please!"

"Cole?" she asked. "Cider?"

"Absolutely."

"Help yourself," she said with a gesture to the food that sat out on the stovetop. He loaded up two plates as she ladled out their cider. By the time she had set their drinks on the table, Cole was putting a fully loaded plate down in front of her.

"It smells amazing," he said as he sat down around the corner from her. "All of it."

Andrea left her cider to cool and poured each of them a glass of red wine.

"To the chef," Cole said, lifting his glass.

"To Mom," Jeffrey agreed, raising his mug of cider.

"To good food and good wine." Andrea clinked her wine glass against the mug and Cole's glass before taking a sip.

Rich earthiness washed over her tongue, the perfect companion to tonight's roast. "This is delicious."

"*This* is delicious," Cole mumbled through a mouth full of food. He swallowed and asked, "How did you make Brussels sprouts taste so good?"

"Brussels sprouts always taste good," Jeffrey said, and Cole barked out a laugh.

"You've never had them boiled. Or from a can."

Jeffrey wrinkled his nose. "They come in cans?"

Cole raised his thick eyebrows and looked at Andrea, dark eyes twinkling. "Lucky kid."

She just grinned and ate a bite of the sprouts in question. They were dark brown and crispy like a roasted marshmallow and nearly as sweet. Sometimes when she was cooking for one, she would just eat a whole pan of roasted Brussels sprouts topped with lemon and Parmesan.

There was a long silence as they each dug into their food, and Andrea cast out for a question that would get the conversation flowing.

"How long have you lived in Cherry Blossom Point, Cole?"

"Long time." He took a huge bite of the pot roast and muttered something that sounded like *delicious* with a choice expletive in front.

"We just moved here," Jeffrey volunteered.

"What do you think?" When Cole asked the question, it seemed to blend into a single word.

"I love it here," Jeffrey enthused. "The survival school is so cool."

Cole nodded. "Jack's a good man."

"He and Wyatt saved my life," Jeffrey confided in a tone

that mixed the gravity of his grandfather's death with the thrill of adventure and the slight hero worship he felt toward his rescuers. He launched into the story, and Cole listened attentively as he ate, giving Andrea an occasional glance that seemed to convey his understanding of how intensely traumatic the whole ordeal must have been for her.

"That's quite the story," he acknowledged when Jeffrey paused to shovel potatoes into his mouth. The boy nodded vigorously as he chewed.

"That's what I'm going to do when I grow up," he said as soon as his mouth was empty. "I'm going to save people."

Andrea's heart flip-flopped in her chest as an increasingly familiar torrent of emotions duked it out within her. She loved her brave boy so much that it hurt.

Jeffrey's cheeks colored, and he looked down. "It sounds stupid when I say it out loud."

"No," Cole said. "Nothing stupid about wanting to help people in trouble. And if you want to learn everything you'll need to help people who get stuck in the mountains, well, you're in the perfect place for that."

Andrea watched him as he spoke, riveted by the low rumble of his voice. That had to be the most she had ever heard him say all at once. She was touched.

After Jeffrey and Cole had helped her clear the table and load the dishwasher, Andrea sent them into the living room to relax while she whipped up some cream to go with the pumpkin pie she had made earlier that day. The pie had come out perfect—she had baked the extra filling in a smaller dish and eaten it for lunch before it had even had the chance to cool. When the cream started to thicken, she paused to add cinnamon, nutmeg, and a splash of amaretto. Without the whir of the mixer, she could hear Cole and Jeffrey talking in the next room.

"So you tripped and fell, huh?" Cole's voice rumbled through the open door.

"Yeah," Jeffrey said, hardly audible.

Cole grunted in acknowledgement, and there was a moment of silence. Then he asked, "What really happened?"

Another beat of silence.

"This guy pushed me into my locker," Jeffrey admitted softly. Andrea's hand flew to her chest, and she took a few steps toward the door, but then she paused when her son spoke again. "Don't tell my mom, okay? It would just stress her out, and there's nothing she can do about it."

Cole was quiet, and Andrea found herself hoping that he wasn't about to give her young son terrible advice like saying he should pick a fight to show the other guy he could handle himself. Staying quiet in the kitchen was torture, but some deep voice told her to wait and listen. And at this point in her motherhood journey, Andrea was pretty good at listening to her gut.

"Starting at a new school is tough," Cole said at last. "You'll find your people soon, and it'll get easier. Once you surround yourself with people who treat you right, the other ones tend to fall away. Just avoid the jerks and focus on making friends with the good ones."

"What am I supposed to do in the meantime?"

"Don't let them get under your skin. Or at least don't let them see that it bothers you. If you don't take the bait, they'll probably lose interest. Stay out of their way if you can. But if they don't leave you alone, if things do get physical again, you need to tell your mom the truth. Okay?"

"She'll get upset," Jeffrey muttered. "She doesn't need to be worrying about me more than she does already."

"She's a smart lady," Cole told him. "And she's very tough, too. She can handle it."

"Okay. Thanks."

"You promise to come clean if that kid pulls a stunt like this again?"

"Yeah, I promise."

"Good man."

Warm gratitude settled into Andrea's chest as she stepped back to the counter and started her hand mixer back up. It worried her that Jeffrey hadn't come to her for advice, and it worried her even more than he had outright lied to her, but she was braced for all kinds of bumps and bruises as they headed into the teen years. Cole had given him good advice, and she wasn't going to make Jeffrey feel any worse by bringing it up.

The whipped cream reached the perfect consistency, and she called her son and their guest in for dessert.

"Yesss," Jeffrey hissed when he saw what she had made. "Pumpkin pie."

"It looks great," Cole said. "Though I don't think anything could beat that apple pie you made."

"Just wait. She makes the *best* whipped cream you have ever tasted in your life."

Andrea chuckled and set two fat slices of pie on the table and grabbed the third for herself, plunking the bowl of whipped cream down with her other hand. "Does anyone want more cider?"

"Yes please!" Jeff said, already spooning whipped cream

onto his slice of pie. The white was quickly eclipsing the generous slice of pumpkin.

"You sit down," Cole told Andrea. "I'll get it."

She settled into a chair and helped herself to the whipped cream as Cole labeled warm cider into three mugs. He brought them to the table and swiped a clean spoon through the whipped cream to taste it, then looked at Andrea with the same wide-eyed expression that the Brussels sprouts had elicited.

"My God, woman." Cole sat down heavily and topped his pumpkin pie with whipped cream. "You are ruining all other foods for me."

"Peanut butter crackers don't set a very high bar," she said lightly.

"True enough."

They settled into a comfortable silence as they savored the pumpkin pie, and Jeffrey was up out of his seat before he had even swallowed his last bite. He slotted his plate into the dishwasher and then said, "Ronan texted me asking if we could get on our old Minecraft server for a while. I've got like an hour before I need to get ready for bed. Okay if I tell him yes?"

So much for *Stranger Things*. Andrea knew it was only a matter of time before the nights that Jeffrey spent alone or with friends outweighed the number of nights that he spent with her. But at the same time, she was grateful that he was still in touch with friends from his old school.

"Yeah, that's fine."

"Thanks, Mom!"

Then it was just her and Cole. Their eyes met for a split

second, and Andrea looked away involuntarily. She picked up their empty plates and carried them over to the dishwasher, trying to avoid the urge to break the silence with useless chatter. Would he say something about his conversation with Jeffrey? Or would Cole keep her son's confidence?

"How you holding up?"

She winced and shrugged. "Okay. Just waiting to hear if the blood belonged to Wren. You?"

"I've been better," he admitted. "I can't help but wonder if things would've turned out different if I'd seen the sock myself two days earlier."

"You can't blame yourself," she said softly. "You had no way of knowing."

"Sometimes logic doesn't matter, you know?"

She did know. She'd spent countless hours wishing she hadn't allowed Jeff and her dad to go backpacking that day.

"Well," Cole said, his voice close enough that it startled her. How did such a broad-shouldered man move so quietly? "I appreciate your hospitality, but I should get going."

Andrea straightened up and turned to face him. Cole stood less than a foot away, and when she looked into his dark eyes, Andrea felt a sudden urge to close the space. The thought startled her so much that she took a step back, bumping into her kitchen counter. Cole mirrored her, taking a half step backwards.

"Thank you for dinner. That was the best meal I've had in a very long time."

Andrea nodded dumbly, suddenly the quieter one of the two. When had that happened?

"I can see myself out," Cole offered.

And then he was gone.

16

LENA

"How did you sleep, bud?" Owen asked, setting down some eggs and toast in front of Sam. A significant number of their meals were still takeout, but their fridge and pantries were always fully stocked these days. It helped that Lena worked with so many local foodies, and her sisters were always going out of their way to drop off kid-friendly meals like chicken pot pies or Monster Mac'n'Cheese.

"Fine."

"What was the best part of your day?" Lena tried.

Sam made a vague 'I dunno' noise, his mouth busy with scrambled eggs. Lena shot Owen a glance, and he just shrugged.

"Hey, I was thinking...what do you say we go into school late today? There's something I wanted to show you," Lena said, smiling over the nervous anticipation in her chest.

Sam shrugged, a wary look in his eyes.

"Okay, I guess." He turned his attention back to his food.

Lena had wondered if she would have trouble getting Sam into the car without Addy for the surprise she had planned, but he climbed right in after his breakfast. His easy compliance wasn't particularly reassuring. If anything, it left Lena feeling more worried than before. He'd eaten his breakfast and then followed her out the door with the blank expression that only seemed to disappear for long when he was playing with his baby sister.

He was adrift—not sinking but not swimming, either. Just holding on, exhausted, at the mercy of the current. Lena wanted desperately to pull him out of the water and into the sunshine, but she didn't know how.

Well, that wouldn't stop her from trying. She was determined to be the mother Sam needed, whatever that looked like, and find a way to reach him somehow, however long it took.

Sam raised a hand in farewell to Owen and Addy as they waved him off. Then he just sat still and silent in his seat as they drove across town. Lena bit back a dozen questions that bubbled up in her mind and resisted the urge to grill him about how things were going at school and how he was feeling. Instead, she turned the radio on and let him be quiet.

Lena had been prepared to deal with angry, reactive behavior. She had read so many books on helping kids navigate their emotions, and she had a gut feeling that it would be healthy for Sam to find an outlet for the mountain of grief and fear that weighed on his small shoulders. But their little Sam wasn't acting out at all. He wasn't outwardly angry... just distant. Lena might not know much about parenting, but she'd lived long enough to understand that stuffing feelings down wasn't healthy. If she couldn't find any good books on the subject, the next step would be finding a good therapist. Not necessarily for Sam quite yet—she found it hard to believe that handing him off to yet another stranger would do him any good in his current frame of mind—but for her and Owen at the very least. Someone who could help them through this and give them tools that they could use to help Sam.

Nerves buzzed under Lena's skin as she approached Harry's Tow Trucks. She had spoken to the owner on the phone, offering to pay her usual hourly rate, and Harriet had agreed to give Sam a tour. Sam sat up a bit when they passed the first tow truck, and Lena bit back a grin. When she parked along the curb, he gave her a quick, wide-eyed look.

"I've always wanted to learn more about tow trucks," she said in a carefully casual tone, "and my new friend Harriet offered us a tour of her place. What do you think?"

He stared at her for a couple seconds, looking more awake and aware than she had seen him since, well, almost ever. Fully present. His voice was still cautious and quiet when he asked, "Are we going to ride on one?"

Lena grinned. "Yeah, we can do that."

Sam was out the door like a shot, walking down the sidewalk at a pace that was nearly a run. Lena chuckled as she hurried to lock her car and catch up with him. There was a small reception area, but Sam headed straight for the open garage door. There was a mechanic on the property, and Sam gazed in wonder at a car that had been lifted up above their heads. He was standing a safe distance away, so Lena let him be.

Sam stood watching the mechanic work for a solid ten minutes. When he finally looked over his shoulder at Lena, she asked, "Are you ready to see some tow trucks?"

Sam smiled at her. "Yeah."

He *smiled.*

At *her.*

Fierce emotions rose in Lena's throat, threatening to let loose a stream of happy tears, but she was *not* about to scare Sam with a sudden outpouring of emotion. She just clapped him gently on the shoulder the way she had seen Owen do and pointed to a door off to the right.

They walked into the front room, where a receptionist who was talking on the phone greeted them with a wave and a smile. They stood and waited, but before she got off of her call, a man Lena's height hurried through and greeted them with a grin.

"Hi, are you Lena?"

"That's me," she confirmed.

"I'm Jimmy." With a thick beard and a plaid shirt, the man looked like a diminutive lumberjack. His voice was warm and welcoming, and his eyes sparkled when he looked at Sam. "And you must be Sam. Harriet told me you two would be coming in. She's out with our biggest truck, but there's still plenty for me to show you. Should we start with the garage?"

"Yeah!" Sam's voice came out so loud and excited that Lena thought of Aiden, her exuberant nephew. She made a mental note to find more time to get together with Gemma and the kids. They had been giving each other space, each getting used to their new family dynamics, but it was about time to start building memories between the soon-to-be cousins.

Lena trailed along happily as Jimmy led Sam into the garage and launched into a detailed but kid-friendly explanation of the work that the mechanics were doing. Sam hung on his every word, giving him the occasional friendly glance but mostly staring open-mouthed at the bottom of the car overhead.

"Ready to get to the trucks?" Jimmy asked after a while.

Sam responded with an emphatic "Yes."

Jimmy led them out of the garage, and Lena was touched when Sam glanced over his shoulder to make sure that she was still with them. She gave him a little wave and a smile, following just a few steps behind, and was rewarded with a full-on grin before he turned his attention back to the tow truck operator.

"We have a few different types of tow trucks here," Jimmy said. "Harriet had to take the flatbed truck out about an hour ago, but we've got some others on the lot that are really cool. Have you seen a wheel lift tow truck before?"

"I don't know," Sam said, trotting to keep up with Jimmy's fast-paced walk.

He stopped in front of the first truck and said, "Well, this here is a wheel lift tow truck. This yoke here on the back extends out and under the car, right under the front wheels. Then it lifts up the front of the car and pulls it along with the back wheels still on the ground."

"That is so cool," Sam breathed.

"Right?" Jimmy chuckled and glanced at Lena, amusement twinkling in his eyes. He walked on, and Sam hurried to keep up. "Okay, so this one over here is called an integrated tow truck. It's real powerful, and we can use it to help trucks and buses that break down."

Lena zoned out as Jimmy went into the specifics of how the truck worked. She stood a few feet away, drinking in the look on Sam's face. He was fully present, totally engaged.

He was *happy*.

"And this one here," Jimmy continued as he led them to the last truck on the lot, "is your classic hook and chain tow truck. The hook grabs on to the bumper of a car, and the chains go around the frame to keep it steady. When all that is ready, this boom lifts the front wheels off the ground. This old girl isn't so popular anymore because the chains can do a bit of damage, but we still use her for cars that are totaled— that's cars that are too damaged to fix that we just need to get off the road. She's great for cars that get stuck in mud or in a ditch. She's got a real powerful winch."

Sam asked a few questions that had Jimmy launching off into rescue stories. Lena went to stand next to Sam, more interested in the stories of stranded travelers than she had been in the mechanics of the trucks. Absentmindedly, maybe not even realizing what he was doing, Sam took Lena's hand. Her heart stuttered and sped as she looked down at her foster son, who was still entranced.

"Ready for a ride?" Jimmy asked after a while.

Sam looked up at Lena, wide eyed. "Can we?"

"Absolutely we can," she told him. He rewarded her with a sunny smile and a squeeze of her hand.

"Which truck did you want to take a ride in?" Jimmy asked.

"This one," Sam said without hesitation. "The hook and chain."

"A classic," the man approved. "A man after my own heart. Climb on in."

Sam scrambled up to the center of the bench seat and clipped on a seatbelt that was clearly much younger than the truck itself. Lena climbed in after him and buckled up, and

Jimmy drove them down the road a ways. Sam was practically vibrating with excitement, his legs doing little happy kicks on the high seat.

Jimmy drove off the road and into a lot that held a long line of totaled cars.

"Woah," Sam breathed, looking at the wrecks.

"Pretty gnarly, right?" Jimmy said. "Want to pick one up?"

"Me?" Sam twisted around in his seat so quickly that he would have tumbled off the bench if he wasn't strapped in.

Jimmy chuckled. "Yeah, let's do it."

"We're going to tow a car?" Sam's voice was squeaky with excitement.

"What do you say, Mom?" Jimmy asked. "Should we tow a car?"

Lena waited for Sam to correct him, to say that Lena wasn't his mom, but he didn't. He just gave Lena a cartoonishly wide-eyed, pleading look.

"Of course!" she agreed.

"Thank you!" Sam exclaimed. He bounced up and down with excitement as Jimmy backed up to one of the wrecked cars, and then he practically flew out of the cab in his hurry to help Jimmy with the hook and chains. Lena climbed out of the high cab with a bit more effort and snapped a few pictures while Jimmy led Sam through the whole process of getting a car hooked up.

And then, miracle of miracles as far as Sam was concerned, Jimmy let him work the controls that lifted the car's front tires off the ground. They moved the car to the end of the line, and then Sam got to help with the whole process of unhooking it, still completely engaged.

When they got back to the lot and one of the mechanics took a few minutes to explain something to Sam, Lena tried to hand Jimmy the check she had written that morning.

"Nope, can't take that," Jimmy said cheerfully. "Harriet gave me strict instructions not to accept a dime."

"I can't let you do that," Lena protested.

"Boss's orders. And honestly, I had a blast. It was way more fun than waiting around for a call, and it was great to see your kid having so much fun."

"You have no idea," Lena said, blinking back tears. "He's had a really rough year."

"Wouldn't know it to look at him," Jimmy said, clapping Lena on the arm. "Good job, Mom."

Lena stood dumbfounded as Jimmy walked back to the main office. She went to stand next to Sam. His eyes didn't leave the car engine that he was staring at, but he put his hand in hers again.

"My dad loved to work on cars," Sam said in a casual tone, still watching the mechanic in front of him at work. Lena's stomach dropped.

"Yeah?" she asked, not sure what else to say.

"Yeah. He let me help him sometimes."

"That's really cool."

"Yeah." They stood watching the mechanic work for a few more minutes, and then Sam scratched his chin thoughtfully. "I didn't eat all my breakfast. Maybe we could stop and get a donut before I go to school?"

Lena's heart did a somersault as she blinked back tears of joy. Her son was requesting more time with her.

Miracle of miracles.

"That sounds like a great idea, buddy."

17

ANDREA

ANDREA HOOKED her computer bag over one shoulder and trudged up Bobbie's front walk, slow and bleary-eyed with lack of sleep. Tired as she was, she felt grateful to be out of her house. The handful of mornings that she'd spent working at Bobbie's place weren't strictly necessary—remote meetings would have worked just fine—but they lived so close to each other and both worked in isolation, so talking in person and clacking away at their keyboards together occasionally was a nice change of pace.

"Hi!" Bobbie opened the door before Andrea even knocked. "I heard you pull up."

"Good morning." Andrea greeted her with a weak attempt at a smile.

Bobbie's eyebrows pulled together. "You look like you haven't slept in days. What gives?"

"It's a long story."

"We've got time. Come on in."

Andrea stepped into the warmth of Bobbie's house, and her friend took her laptop bag while she shrugged off her coat. The small home was cozy and comfortable, full of the barely controlled chaos that came with having a baby and a small business. Stacks of papers lined one wall, and there were a dozen baby toys scattered across a quilt on the floor.

"Is Archie napping?" Andrea asked.

"He's off with his daddy for the morning. Do you want some coffee?"

"Please." Andrea followed Bobbie through to the kitchen and accepted the offering. She wrapped her hands around the warm mug with a tired gratitude, letting the warmth of the drink and the kitchen sink into her bones. There was something in the oven, and the little kitchen slash dining room smelled like a bakery. The homeness of it all chipped away at Andrea's defenses, and tears pricked at her eyes.

"So," Bobbie said gently, settling into one of her kitchen chairs and gesturing for Andrea to do the same. "What's up?"

Andrea sighed heavily as she sat down. She took a long sip of coffee, wondering how much backstory to provide. In the end, she jumped right to the point.

"I found a sock in a loaner car. Wren's sock. Probably."

"What?" Bobbie set her mug down with a *thunk* that sent coffee sloshing over the rim. "That was you who found the sock? Oh my God!"

"Yeah." Andrea's voice came out in a croak, and she took another sip of hot coffee. "It was in the car I borrowed from the mechanic, and for a minute I thought that maybe he–" She broke off with a shake of her head. "I snooped around his house. He caught me. It was humiliating. But now we have that image of the guy who *might* have taken Wren."

"Andy, that's huge. It's the first decent lead they've had.

154

They've been running that dark, grainy image over and over. You must be so shaken up."

Andrea nodded. A timer went off on the stove, and Bobbie jumped up.

"Just a sec, sorry." She ran to pull a tray of muffins out of the oven.

"How's the tip line going so far?" Andrea asked.

"Nothing so far." Bobbie walked back to the table and wiped up her spilled coffee before slumping back into her chair. "We always knew it was a long shot. But now, with that drawing and video... That's something, at least."

Andrea nodded. "Hopefully someone will recognize this guy, and this nightmare will be over."

"Her poor mother," Bobbie murmured, wrapping her hands around her coffee mug. "I can't even imagine."

"I can," Andrea said grimly. Bobbie met her eyes and reached out to pat her hand. "It's not the same, but, well, it is in a way. And if I had gone days and days without..." She trailed off and shook her head. "It's the worst kind of torture."

They were quiet for a while, sipping their coffee. The events of the past week loomed large in Andrea's mind. And while she felt that her thoughts and prayers should be with Wren's poor mother, her subconscious kept steering her back toward a certain dark-eyed mechanic.

"Do you know Cole Spivey?" The question was out of her mouth before she had even made a conscious decision to ask it. "The mechanic?"

Bobbie frowned thoughtfully and shook her head. "Only from the stuff on the news about the shop, why?"

Andrea felt her cheeks color. Despite the heavy weight of worry in her heart, a small smile stole over her lips. She looked at her friend and admitted, "I might have a tiny crush on him."

"What?" Bobbie grinned, switching instantaneously from worried mother to gossiping girlfriend. "Tell me everything!"

"I'm not sure if it's just because we weathered a weird, stressful, scary circumstance together...but I really like him. I had him over for dinner—just as a thank you for the car and all."

"Right." Bobbie smirked.

"*Anyway*, he was great with Jeffrey. Who's suddenly telling me to date, by the way. He's old enough to realize it's weird that I spend all my time alone or with him. I guess seeing Wyatt's mom with her new boyfriend put the idea in his head. So he'd be okay with it, I think. But I don't even know if Cole would be interested in dating me anyway," she finished lamely.

Bobbie raised an eyebrow. "I know one way to find out."

"No way! I already made him dinner. I can't ask him out on a second date when I don't even know if our first date was a date."

"Was Jeffrey there?"

"Yeah."

"It doesn't sound like your first date *was* a date."

Andrea sighed. "I did tell him that it was an apology."

"Well, that's–"

"Hello hello!" Marcus called as he opened the front door.

"Back here," Bobbie called. Marcus walked through to the kitchen, and a puzzled frown appeared on Bobbie's face. "Where's Archie?"

"Gemma took him for a couple hours."

"Why?"

"I need to talk to you about something." Marcus had a serious look on his face, and Andrea supposed that was her cue to go.

"I was just leaving anyway," she said. Bobbie gave her a look of surprise, and Andrea responded with a shrug and a small smile. She wasn't in a state to get much work done today, anyhow. "Thanks for the coffee, Bobbie. I'll get next month's columns to you by Monday."

"Do you want to take some muffins to go?" Bobbie asked. "They're blueberry orange."

"I can't say no to that."

"I'll walk you out." Bobbie quickly packed up some muffins and walked Andrea to the front door.

"Thanks again." Andrea reached for the muffins, but Bobbie didn't let go.

"You really like this guy?"

Andrea thought of Cole's stern face and felt another flush of heat in her cheeks. She smiled shyly and admitted, "I feel like a schoolgirl when I think about him."

"So what are you waiting for? You might *feel* like a schoolgirl, but you're a grown-ass woman. Go ask that man on a date."

Andrea chuckled at the younger woman's intensity. "Thanks, Bobbie."

Bobbie handed her the muffins and gave her a quick hug. "Anytime."

"I think you're nice," Andrea said under her breath, pacing outside of Cole's garage. " If you think I'm nice too, maybe we could—Ugh, that's terrible. Besides, he isn't even that nice. He's sort of grumpy a lot of the time. Okay, so, I had a really good time the other night and I was hoping you'd—"

"I was wondering when you'd be back."

Andrea jumped and spun around. Starla was watching her from a few yards away, leaning against the side of the building in the shade.

"I—um—hi," Andrea fumbled.

Starla shook her head and walked toward Andrea. "He's a good one," she said with a sheepish, resigned smile on her face. "Don't hurt him, okay?"

"Okay," Andrea said.

"He's in the garage working on a Mazda. I was just bringing him lunch." She held out a takeout bag and sighed. "You can do it."

Andrea accepted the bag. The food inside was still warm. "Thanks, Starla."

The younger woman shrugged. "I have a lunch date. You kids have fun."

A one-note laugh escaped Andrea's throat. "Thanks."

She found Cole under a car. He slid out and gave her a look remarkably close to a *smile* when he saw her. "Hey there."

"Hi." Andrea held out the bag. "I was tasked with delivering your lunch."

"Were you now?"

"I came by to see if you had time to talk, but if you're too busy—"

"I'm ready for a lunch break. You can join me. I'll even share my meatloaf sandwich with you. Just need to wash my hands. Come on in where it's warm."

"That's a lot of words all in a row," she teased, trying to lighten her anxiety with a joke.

"Are you calling me taciturn?" he asked, deadpan. When Andrea's eyebrows shot up, the side of his mouth quirked up a bit. "Laconic? The strong silent type?"

Andrea smiled softly. "Aren't you?"

"Mostly. But not for lack of vocabulary. Come on." He turned and walked through to the waiting room, disappearing through another door for a minute and coming back with clean hands. As he dug into the sandwich bag, he said, "Meatball sandwich from Marzano's. Best in town."

"Thank you," Andrea said as she accepted her half.

"How are you holding up?" he asked as they sat down to eat.

"Not great," she admitted with a sigh. "On top of the empathy any mother would feel, it brings up a lot of feelings from when Jeffrey was missing."

"I get it. I can't stop thinking about it either. That girl's family. I know what it is to lose a piece of you. I hope to God that girl's mother doesn't have to learn to live without her."

"Me too," Andrea murmured. She gave Cole a questioning look, wondering who he had lost but not wanting to pry.

"My brother," he said in answer to her unspoken question. "My twin. Landon. He died of an overdose five years ago."

"Cole. I'm sorry." Andrea put her hand over his and felt a thrill when he turned his palm up, wrapping his fingers over hers. She was hyper aware of the strong, smooth calluses at the base of his fingers.

"We were close," Cole rumbled after a moment. "I...I still drive his truck sometimes."

Andrea followed his gaze out the window and saw the truck that she had asked—demanded, really—to borrow. No wonder he had been so short with her.

"Some days I'm okay. Others I can hardly stop it from swallowing me whole."

"I feel the same way about my dad." Andrea could hardly get the words out. She swallowed back a rush of tears and took a shaky breath. "Well. Aren't we a pair?"

Cole met her gaze. His stare was intense, but an almost-smile played over his lips. "Are we?"

Andrea let the question sit there for a moment, looking into his eyes. Most of the time, they looked nearly black. Just now, in the light shining through the big front window, they were a clear, deep brown like a glass bottle.

"I've been wondering that myself," she said at last.

"What say we find out? How about dinner this weekend? On me this time. I can't cook for you...not if you value your digestive health, but I have a fancy credit card with a high limit, and I know a good restaurant when I see it."

Andrea smiled. Her hand was still in his, and she gave it a squeeze. "Yeah. Okay. My mom would love to have an excuse to come visit and have some one-on-one time with her grandson." She paused and then said, "Speaking of my son... When were you going to tell me?"

Cole's thick eyebrows furrowed. "Tell you what?"

"About the bullying thing with Jeffrey."

"I wasn't," he said immediately. In a softer voice, he said, "The kid trusted me. I wasn't going to break that trust. I wouldn't do that unless he was in real danger."

Andrea was quiet for a moment, digesting his words. She wondered if she should be annoyed... but instead, it only made her like him more. Cole was a man with bone-deep integrity. The kind of man that a person could depend on. And suddenly, Andrea felt sure.

She didn't care about his lack of social skills, or his cranky nature, or even the gravy on his coveralls. She liked *him*. She liked him a lot.

Andrea leaned in and kissed him dead on the mouth.

Then, without waiting for a reaction, she stood and walked toward the front door.

"Six o'clock on Saturday," she called over her shoulder. "Don't be late!"

18

BOBBIE

BOBBIE'S KNEES bounced nervously as Marcus drove her through town. The trees they passed were skeletal, mostly bare save for a few sad leaves still clinging on. A dozen questions rose in her throat like bile, but she swallowed them all down. Marcus didn't owe her a thing, not after what she had put him through. He had forgiven her—at least he said he had—but the guilt of hiding Archie all through her pregnancy and then through the first few months of their son's life still weighed heavy on her heart.

Marcus had been so distracted lately. Was his patience with her finally wearing thin? Was he ready to jet off overseas and devote himself to a truly worthy cause? Had he found that, despite his best efforts, he could never truly forgive her?

What if she and Archie would never be enough for him?

Marcus pulled into a nice strip mall and parked, and Bobbie eyed a fish and chips shop with distrust. Was he planning to soften her up with dinner before he broke the news?

She sat frozen in her seat while Marcus climbed out of the car.

He loves you, Bobbie told herself, trying to calm that frightened little girl inside who was still terrified that everyone she loved would leave her sooner or later. *Marcus loves you in spite of everything, and he loves Archie more than anything in this world. Even if his work takes him overseas, we'll get through it. We're a family now. That's never going to change.*

"Come on!" Marcus said, opening Bobbie's door for her. There was a wide grin on his face, and Bobbie's heart sped. Even as scared as she was, it warmed her heart to see him so excited.

"Where are we going?" she asked.

"Right here!" Marcus gestured to the empty storefront directly in front of the space he had parked in. He towed her to the door, pulled a set of keys from his pocket, and unlocked it.

"I don't understand."

"I'm starting my own practice!" Marcus flipped on the lights and revealed the shell of a waiting room. It was bare but spacious, with a typical reception desk and window built into one wall.

"Your own practice," Bobbie echoed. She leaned into him, so shocked that she could hardly stand. "You're staying?"

"Of course I'm staying." Marcus leaned away for a second, just long enough to look down and see the fear in Bobbie's eyes. Then he half laughed and pulled her into his arms. "Oh, Bobbie. I'm so sorry. Did I scare you? I'm sorry I've been so distracted lately. I didn't want to tell you until I was sure. I didn't know if I would be able to get out of my next assignment without letting my team down, but I found someone to take my place in Mozambique. And I just secured this space yesterday. I have a few investors lined up, enough to get started."

He released his grip on her shoulders but took hold of her hand and pulled her through to the hallway, showing her the clinic rooms and office space.

"I want to focus on pediatrics," Marcus said as they toured the small clinic, "but I'm open to developing more of a small-town style family practice. We'll see what the town needs. I'm thinking that I can set up free clinic days once or twice a month for people who can't afford to see a doctor as often as they need to."

"No more Africa?" Bobbie asked, her voice made mousy by a combination of relief and guilt. What if he came to resent her from pulling him away from his life's work?

Marcus took a deep breath and paused his whirlwind tour to look Bobbie in the eye.

"I'm right where I want to be." He sealed the statement with a kiss, then straightened up and smiled. "I'm not giving up on overseas work. Just pressing pause. Someday, when Archie's in school, I might do some stints abroad for a month or two at a time. But for now, I don't want to miss a thing. And I think there's a lot of good that I can do here."

Bobbie's relief deepened, sinking into her bones, and she squeezed his hand. "I know there is."

"Come look." Marcus led her back into the waiting room and pointed to one of the walls. "I want to knock out part of this wall and put in a big aquarium, low enough for little kids to be able to watch the fish. We can set up a play area in this corner here and bench seating right here."

"You're excited," Bobbie said with a little laugh. He was truly passionate about starting his own practice. Marcus was ready to settle down, but he wasn't *settling*. This was what he really wanted. He didn't resent her. He wanted to build a life with her. Joy rushed through Bobbie's body, and she wrapped her arms tightly around Marcus's waist.

"Of course I'm excited! Are you kidding me? My own practice! I want to focus on root cause stuff, like nutrition and movement and sunshine. Really help families build a strong foundation for their kids' health. Maybe run some workshops on prenatal nutrition too."

"I love that."

"I love you," Marcus said, planting a kiss on the top of her head. "I'm not going anywhere, Bobbie. Let's go home."

A few quick texts confirmed that Gemma was happy to keep Archie a while longer, so Bobbie and Marcus drove straight home. When they got there, Marcus went into the kitchen and came back with a bottle of champagne.

"We have the house to ourselves," he said as he worked out the cork. "I thought you might want to celebrate."

"Of course!" Bobbie let out a shriek of laughter as the bottle opened with a loud pop.

"I forgot the glasses," Marcus laughed as he snatched a baby blanket up off the couch and caught the flow of bubbles.

"I'll get them."

"Here." Marcus handed over the bottle. "I'll start a fire."

"Sounds good. We still have some of those quick-start logs."

When Bobbie came back with two glasses of champagne,

Marcus was kneeling in front of a happy little fire. And when he turned to her, still kneeling, she nearly dropped their drinks.

He was holding a tiny black box.

"There was one more thing I've been wanting to talk to you about." Marcus opened the box, and a diamond sparkled at her from atop a golden ring. "It might seem fast, but Bobbie... I've loved you since we were kids. I asked my mom to give me her mother's ring when we were down there, and she told me she always thought that I would give it to you. Ever since we were little."

Bobbie sank down next to him and carefully set their drinks down on the floor. She was speechless, but she held her hand out and let Marcus slide his family ring onto her finger.

It was a perfect fit.

"I don't want to live in separate houses anymore," he told her, holding her hand in both of his. "I want to be with you and Archie every morning and every night. I want to build a life together and watch our son grow. I'm all in, Bobbie. Will you marry me?"

Two tears escaped Bobbie's eyes even as she pulled him in for a kiss.

"Yes," she said in a rush, realizing that she still hadn't given him an answer. "Yes, Marcus, I'll marry you. I'll live with you. I'm all in."

Marcus laughed in a way that came close to a sob. He took her face in both hands and kissed her again, long and hard. Then he leaned back and smiled at her.

"Would it be okay if we called my mom and dad? She

made me promise I would FaceTime them as soon as the ring was on your finger."

"Sure," Bobbie laughed, brushing away her tears. "Just let me clean up real quick."

"You're gorgeous," Marcus protested, but Bobbie stood up and trotted toward the bathroom.

"I just need a splash of cold water and some lip gloss! And we have to call my sisters after we get off the phone with your parents!"

She went into the bathroom to wash her face, but a notification from her phone made her pause. Someone had just left a message from an unknown number, and Bobbie felt a sinking feeling in her gut. What if it was the tip line? She couldn't *not* check it.

So far, nothing helpful had come in. One crackpot had called to ramble about how he hated Graham's politics and thought he was part of the Illuminati. And then some woman wanted to tell them about the janitor at the children's school had never *done* or *said* anything inappropriate, but the guy gave her "bad vibes." Still, if there was even the tiniest chance that someone had called with a real lead...

Champagne could wait. Bobbie unlocked her phone and pressed play.

"*Hello?*" a woman said in a shaky voice. "*Hi...Um, this is Muriel Sinclair. I live over on Crabapple Road, and I saw your little pamphlet about the tip line for poor Wren Hazelton. I've been hemming and hawing about making this call since I saw the news this morning, but I can't get it out of my head. You know that video they've been showing of the man at that garage? Well, I think he might be my landscaper.*"

There was a long pause, and Bobbie's heart raced.

"Ohhh, I do hope I'm not telling tales out of school," Muriel fretted. *"The video footage isn't very clear, and you can't see much of his face... look, I would hate to get someone in trouble if I'm wrong, but I have an eye for faces. Anyway, I wouldn't forgive myself if I didn't say anything."* Muriel took a deep breath and continued, *"His name is Ivan, and he works for Petrullo's Landscaping."*

Bobbie braced herself against the counter with both hands. She was afraid to get hopeful, but something told her that this was the first real tip they'd gotten, and it could change everything..

"Marcus?" she called, straightening. "Come here. You need to hear this."

19

FALLYN

FALLYN RUBBED AT HER TEMPLES, blinking repeatedly to soothe the exhaustion-fueled dryness in her eyes. Her mind had been churning at full speed since their last shocking visit with Graham Hazelton, trying to figure out the best course of action, making sleep nearly impossible. They'd ruled out getting the police involved, knowing they'd insist on being present for the money drop-off. If the kidnapper got wind of that, it was impossible to say what might become of Wren. But leaving Graham Hazelton, of all people, to handle this alone didn't seem like a wise idea either. Putting herself in Alicia's shoes, she knew she wouldn't want him to be the one in charge of something this important. She'd watched enough clips of him in the press from his first campaign to know that he sometimes acted impulsively, breaking that carefully cultivated air of posh civility and snapping at reporters in anger. Oftentimes, the things he said led to sheepish staffers having to come back and clean up his messes with half-apologies and claims of "gotcha journalism."

And, while he played the part of a concerned father, his life largely seemed devoid of any indication that he had a child at all. Until she'd seen his concern firsthand when he'd learned of the blood found in the Subaru, she'd almost wondered if he felt any attachment to Wren whatsoever. Luckily, early this morning, they'd learned that, while the sock was determined to be Wren's, the blood?

Was not.

Yet another reason to let it all unfold as if they'd never seen the ransom note.

Only they had...

And if they did nothing, and Graham screwed this up–

"It feels like our hands are tied. Damned if we do, damned if we don't," she groaned, not for the first time. She winced slightly as she took a swig of her lukewarm coffee.

"Well, we don't have long to worry about it," David replied grimly, glancing at his watch. "The kidnapper should be in touch with Graham at any time now to set up the drop. This could all be over soon."

Fallyn opened her mouth to reply but was interrupted by buzzing on the table next to her. Her heart thumped with anticipation as she grabbed the phone and flipped it to look at the number, but she didn't recognize the caller.

She answered anyway.

"Hello?"

"Hi, is this Fallyn Rappaport?" a woman asked on the other side of the line.

"It is," Fallyn replied.

"Ah, great. I'm Bobbie Pardue, from the *Cherry Blossom Bee*, and I'm calling about a message we received on our tip line."

Recognition washed over Fallyn. Their hostess, Ellie, had mentioned the tip line in passing to them, and she'd seen the paper around town. "Oh, hi Bobbie," she said, sitting up a little straighter, "mind if I put you on speaker? My partner is here too, and I figure we may as well both hear about it in one go."

"No problem at all," Bobbie said.

Fallyn covered the receiver and whispered to Shaw, "It's the lady from the local newspaper. They got a tip from that tip line."

She tapped on the speakerphone and set it down on the coffee table between them.

"Bobbie, may I ask...have you contacted the police with this yet?" Fallyn said.

"Yeah, I just got off of the phone with them, actually. I'm trying to make sure everyone on this case has access to all the information," Bobbie replied, clearly distraught. "This poor little girl needs as many people looking for her as possible. I wouldn't have bothered you with it if I didn't get the feeling that it could be a major lead."

"We're happy you thought of us," Fallyn said. They'd spent the majority of the last day at a standstill, and this new piece of information could be the thing to shake things up and give them an actual path forward.

"The call was actually recorded on voicemail. I'll play it for you now."

"Hello?" a woman said in a shaky voice. *"Hi...Um, this is Muriel Sinclair. I live over on Crabapple Road, and I saw your little pamphlet about the tip line for poor Wren Hazelton. I've been hemming and hawing about making this call since I saw the news this morning, but I can't get it out of*

my head. You know that video they've been showing of the man at that garage? Well, I think he might be my landscaper. Ohhh, I do hope I'm not telling tales out of school. The video footage isn't very clear and you can't see much of his face... look, I would hate to get someone in trouble if I'm wrong, but I have an eye for faces. Anyway, I wouldn't forgive myself if I didn't say anything."

There was a pause, and Fallyn's back straightened even further as her hand darted automatically to her pen.

"His name is Ivan, and he works for Petrullo's Landscaping."

Fallyn jotted the information down on autopilot, but her eyes were closed as the gears in her mind began to grind.

Where had she heard that name before?

Petrullo's.

Petrullo's Landscaping.

Before Bobbie could speak again, the memory hit Fallyn like a brick between the eyes.

"'Quality lawn care for quality people,'" she whispered.

"'Scuse me?" Bobbie asked.

"Sorry, nothing. Um... Bobbie, thank you so much for that information. I can't tell you how grateful we are that you reached out." She shot Shaw a significant look, and he raised his brows in question. "We're going to let you go so we can try to run with this. Thanks again, and please, feel free to call any time day or night if you hear anything else that you think might be of interest."

Bobbie agreed and said her goodbyes before disconnecting.

"What gives?" Shaw demanded.

"Petrullo's Landscaping," she murmured, typing the words quickly into her phone's search bar.

"Yeah, I heard that, but—"

She turned the phone toward him, showing the picture of one of their trucks, and he nodded slowly, eyes wide.

"A truck like that was parked in Graham Hazelton's driveway the first time we visited."

Fallyn nodded. "It makes me wonder if Graham hasn't been a part of this from the start."

Shaw squinted dubiously, flipping open his laptop as he spoke. "Just as likely that this Ivan guy saw Wren firsthand at the house, noticed the kind of bread Hazelton is working with, and identified it as an opportunity."

"Why steal her from her mother's house?"

Shaw shrugged. "Easier to get in and out of. Less secure, for sure, and only her and the kid at home rather than a fully staffed house."

"Agreed," Fallyn said, clenching her jaw, "but my gut tells me it's more than that." She turned to Shaw and blew out a sigh. "Something is seriously off about this whole thing. I know it in my bones."

He paused for a long moment and then started tapping away at his keyboard again. "Well, I know better than to disregard your Spidey sense. Oh! Check it out. It looks like Petrullo's has their Facebook instant messenger set up and use it for booking appointments," he said.

Fallyn considered that and then nodded. "Let's ask to make an appointment with this Ivan guy. We can say he was recommended to us by a friend or something."

He clicked away at the keys, then turned back toward her. "Do you think it's time to tell the cops about the note?"

Fallyn chewed at her cheek and then shook her head. "What if they show up, guns blazing, and cause Wren to be harmed? I can't live with that."

They were down to the final hours that would determine the fate of both Wren and her kidnapper. They couldn't afford to make any mistakes.

"Check it out." Shaw turned his laptop in her direction, gesturing for her to read the reply he'd gotten from Petrullo's.

Hello and welcome to Petrullo's! We love working with new customers, and we have plenty of excellent landscapers, but Ivan hasn't worked here since the week before last. How about we schedule you for an appointment, ten percent off, and we'll find you another team member who is just as capable?

An icy chill skated up the back of her neck. How could they be sure that Ivan was the same man in the picture without blowing the lid off this and potentially causing him to panic and hurt Wren?

There was only one person that might have the answer, who she knew she could trust not to breathe a word of it to anyone, and she prayed it was the right move.

She sighed, turning to Shaw as she stood up from her chair.

"I think we need to pay Alicia Hazelton another visit."

"Come on in," Alicia said in a monotone, gesturing for them to follow her through the door. Her face was pale, and her freckled cheeks were stretched drum tight, like she hadn't eaten since the last time they'd seen her.

Fallyn and Shaw followed her to the dining room, and Fallyn pulled out her recorder and notebook. "As you know, a local paper put together a tip line for people to call to report anything they think might help the case," Fallyn began.

Alicia nodded in recognition. "Yes. The *Cherry Blossom Bee*."

"We don't want to get your hopes up, but the owner may have received a piece of information that could help, but it needs to remain confidential," Fallyn said.

Alicia nodded slowly. "Yes, of course."

"A woman identified the man from the video as a man named Ivan. He works at a place called Petrullo's Landscaping. Does the name ring a bell?"

Alicia frowned thoughtfully. "We used them at our old house, and I've seen the truck at Graham's new place a couple times when I was dropping Wren off for visitation." She paused for a moment, looking up with a puzzled expression. "Wait–" Her eyes widened with realization. "Graham knows him. He knows Ivan. Oh my God, I didn't recognize his picture on the news, but now that I have a face to match it to... I was already starting to drink at the time and had pretty much checked out when it came to anything except Birdie. Graham was out there talking to him a lot for a while, having him put some fruit trees in and add a bunch of fancy lighting around the shrubs. They were chatty. I remember him asking Graham for some stock tips. He was nice to Birdie. Dear God, he could've been watching her... hunting her for months. What if he–" She broke off with a shattered sob, and Fallyn couldn't take it anymore.

She sent Shaw a quick glance, and he nodded. Then she leaned forward and took Alicia's hand.

"Alicia, I need to tell you something, but you have to promise it will stay between us. Can you do that for me?"

The other woman pressed a trembling hand over her mouth and nodded, trying not to crumble.

"Graham recently received a ransom note from the kidnapper. Not only that, it included proof of life."

Shaw already had a copy of the photo at the ready and handed his cell phone to Alicia. She let out a cry and slumped into a heap, never taking her eyes from the image in front of her.

"Oh my God! Oh, my sweet baby!"

Fallyn blinked back her own tears and tried to stay focused. "Supposedly, Graham will be handing over the money tonight. Which means–"

"Birdie could be home tomorrow?! Oh my God, I have to call Linda! No. I can't tell anyone!" Her shock and joy slowly morphed into something else. "Wait...Why didn't he tell me? Why didn't Graham show me this?" she demanded, her voice shaking with fury now.

"Because the note explicitly tells him not to share it with anyone."

"I'm her mother. He would know I'd never tell a soul if it put her at risk. He showed you two."

"He didn't," Fallyn admitted with a shake of her head. "I saw the corner of it sticking out from beneath something on his desk. I made the decision to investigate further."

"Thank God you did," the woman murmured, gazing lovingly back down at the photo again. "So now what?"

"Well," Fallyn said, settling back against her chair, "that's partly up to you. We've been driving ourselves crazy trying to figure out what to do here."

"We can't tell the police. Promise me," Alicia pleaded, panic making her voice go shrill. "If she was safe this whole time and then—"

"I do think once the kidnapper has the ransom money, he will likely bring Wren to the pickup location and then leave town, if not the state, immediately. He practically admits it in the note. And now that his face is circulating, it seems even more likely. I doubt he would stick around until tomorrow to monitor the pickup point."

"Nope. If you tell the police, they will surely want to be part of the whole process. They'll try to mark the bills, be hiding somewhere at the money drop so they can catch the guy." Alicia shook her head adamantly, clutching Shaw's phone more tightly in her hand. "No freaking way. No cops. Not an option. I want this bastard caught, but I want my daughter home alive a billion times more. No cops," she repeated again, her jaw set tight.

"Then you trust Graham to handle this alone?"

"Not on your life," Alicia shot back. "But I trust you two. And I trust myself. I agree, it's unlikely that this Ivan will stay once he's got his money, so let's the three of us tail Graham tomorrow."

Shaw was already shaking his head, but a desperate Alicia continued on.

"I won't make a peep, I swear. Just so long as I can see that he's got her and she's safe, I don't care if he takes the credit for rescuing her. We'll come back here like it never happened and wait for him to bring her home."

Shaw was doing his level best to discuss the pros and cons of following Graham and convince Alicia why her presence would only be a hindrance, but Fallyn barely heard him. Her mind was racing as the last piece of the puzzle slipped into place.

Gotcha.

20

LENA

"Good man," Owen said as Sam pulled a thick sweater over his head. "Now put these plastic overalls on over the wool pants."

"Will they be here soon?" Sam asked as he pulled on his hand-me-down snowsuit. "If I have to wear all this inside for more than a minute, I might suffocate to death before they get here."

Owen chuckled. "Gemma texted when she left, so they should be here any minute."

"We can wait for them outside," Lena offered as she laced up her boots.

"Okay." Sam gave her a weak smile and turned back to Owen. "You're not coming?"

"I'm going to sit this one out and catch up with my sister. We'll keep warm with the babies, but we'll be able to see all your antics through the back window. And you and me can go to the big hill behind the school this weekend, yeah?"

"Yeah, okay." Sam sat on the floor and pulled his baby

sister into his lap, where she let out a happy shriek and tried to bite the metal buttons off of his snowsuit. "Addy can't come?"

"Today's just for the big kids," Lena told him.

And that includes me, she added silently, almost laughing at herself. Gemma and Owen had years of snow days with Liam and Aiden under their belts, and they were more than happy to stay cozy with their baby girls while the big kids played. Lena, on the other hand, was probably more excited than Sam to get out and enjoy this glorious snow day. These were the moments childhood was made of, and where Sam was concerned, Lena had already missed so many. She wasn't going to let any more potential childhood memories slip by if she could help it.

"They're here!" Sam jumped up from the floor when Gemma's car passed by the front window. He passed Addy to Owen and ran out the door. Lena followed with his snow jacket and hat, accepting a quick kiss from Owen on her way out the door.

"Have fun, love. We'll have hot drinks waiting."

Lena stilled for a moment, looking up into the eyes of her best friend. She had everything she'd ever wanted. And it wasn't easy—some days were so, so hard—but good Lord, it was beautiful.

"Is this real life?" she asked playfully. Without waiting for an answer, she kissed him hard on the mouth, dropped a kiss on Addy's head, and went outside, closing the door against the cold.

"Woah!" Sam exclaimed, fully excited now that the older kids were here. He was staring open-mouthed as Gemma pulled a two-person sled from the back of her car, and he didn't resist when Lena helped him into his fat winter coat and pulled a hat down over his ears. Lena herself was so thoroughly bundled that she was nearly a perfect sphere. She had no intention of letting the cold drive her inside before the kids were ready to call it quits.

Zoe and Aiden came tumbling out and each grabbed a circular saucer-style sled, and Liam hopped out of the front seat holding a plastic bag.

"What's that?" Sam asked. He had been shy of his soon-to-be cousins at first but was feeling more comfortable around them after several rounds of pizza and video games.

"Carrots, raisins, some old hats... everything we need for snowmen!"

Lena saw Sam's smile dim in a familiar way. He had been with them long enough now for her to guess at why—nearly every time something happened to remind him of his parents, his light dimmed. There were rare occasions—like their tow truck day—that he was able to mention his parents in a neutral way. But more often than not, the merest mention of them gave Lena a glimpse into the chasm of grief that Sam was still clawing his way out of. She hoped that someday they would be able to honor his parents, to talk about them in an everyday way that brought comfort instead of pain. But it was still too new, too raw.

"Everything okay?" Gemma asked. She shoved her car door closed with one foot and went to stand next to Lena, holding Cara in a big fuzzy blanket that covered her from head to toe.

"Everything's great," Lena said brightly. "You two go in where it's warm. I've got this."

"Thanks, Lena. See you in a bit. Have fun!" she called to her crew.

"Where's the hill?" Zoe demanded, brandishing her purple saucer sled like a shield.

"This way." Lena led them around the side of her house, crunching through the fresh snow. "Come on!"

There was a perfect little sledding hill in Lena's backyard, though she had never actually used it for that purpose. It wasn't as tall or as steep as the popular hills around town, but it had a long slope that was clear of trees, and she was willing to bet that the kids could get some decent speed out of that gentle slope.

Zoe led the charge up the little hill with Aiden and Liam close behind. Lena grabbed the old wooden sled that Owen had fixed up, and she and Sam followed the other kids up the hill. At the top, she caught Liam eying her sled.

"Want to trade?" she offered. Zoe and Aiden were already racing down the slope on their saucers, their shrieking laughter hanging over the tracks they made in the fresh snow.

"Sure!" Liam hopped onto the smaller sled and took off.

Lena turned to Sam and smiled. "Ready?"

"Yeah." There was a nervous edge to his smile, but he took a few steps forward. Below, Zoe and Aiden were already racing back up the hill. "Will you steer?"

"Sure thing. You sit up front." She sat on the back of the sled and let Sam get settled in front of her. The cap that Beth had knit him was soft against her cheek. Lena had never held Sam in her lap, never cuddled him the way she had loved on his sister for countless hours since they had arrived. So this moment, wrapping her padded body protectively around his, was about as close to perfect as life got.

She pushed off, relishing the sound of his laughter and the feeling of her foster son leaning back into her as they sped down the slope. It was over far too soon, but the joy in his face as he tumbled off of the sled was everything.

"Can we go again?" he asked.

"Absolutely we can."

Lena lost track of how many times they went up and down the little hill. The combination of sleds and people changed every time, and racing Sam in the saucers was every bit as much fun as sharing a sled. He was scared of taking his own down alone, but he flew down in the saucers about a dozen times and shared the big sled with everyone at least once as the other kids took turns with his wooden one.

Watching Sam climb aboard with his big cousins warmed Lena's heart. As far as he was concerned, he was putting his life in their hands. And she was fully aware of what a tremendous honor that was.

Finally, when they all sat at the bottom at the same time, too tired to climb up the hill again, Zoe suggested a change of pace.

"Let's make snow angels!"

"That's baby stuff," Aiden protested through a mouthful of snow. He was eating handfuls of it to slake his thirst, and there was a little goatee of melting powder all around his mouth.

"It is not!" Zoe shouted.

"Aiden's just afraid you can make a better one than he can," Liam said. His brother's already-rosy cheeks turned a darker shade of pink.

"No! You know what? I'm gonna make a snow *devil*." Aiden stalked off to a flat patch of snow and threw himself backwards. He lay there for a minute and then shouted, "Someone help me up!"

Sam giggled and ran over to give Aiden a hand so that he could get up without wrecking the print he had made in the snow. Nearby, Zoe was busy making a snow angel.

"Liam, where's the snowman stuff?" Aiden demanded. He spotted the bag and ran over to claim two carrots, which he used to add a long tail to his snow print. Then he carefully set them on top of the head to make two long horns. He spun around and threw his fists in the air, giving his brother a triumphant smile. "Snow devil!"

"Whatever," Liam said. "I'm making a snowman."

"I'll help!" Zoe jumped up from her snow angel, quick and limber as an acrobat despite her thick snowsuit, and the three kids worked together to build a snowman. Sam hung back, prodding listlessly at a small patch of ice with his boot.

"Are you okay?" Lena asked him. She braced her hands on her knees, leaning down so that her eyes were level with his, but he didn't look at her. Just kept kicking at that patch of ice.

"Yeah."

"Are you getting tired?"

Sam shook his head. He looked over at the snowman that was slowly coming together and said, "Me and my mom used to make snow people. Big ones and kids and everything. Like a family."

"That sounds like fun," Lena said softly. She straightened up and put a gloved hand on his shoulder. "Do you want to make a snowkid?"

"Not really."

"How about something else? Have you ever made a snow fort?"

"No."

"Do you want to?"

"Sure."

He wasn't exactly enthusiastic, but she'd take it. They turned their backs on the snowman and started on a fort, working side by side in companionable silence. The further along they got, the more the last of the tension in him seemed to drain away.

"Ahoy there!" Owen called out as he crunched across the snow. "Aren't you lot tired yet?"

"Not even a little bit!" Zoe yelled.

"Frozen in your boots?"

"Nope!" Aiden shouted.

"Aiden, your ma saw you eating snow and figured someone should bring you some provisions." He held up a thermos and a stack of plastic cups. "I've got some warm cider."

"Thanks, Uncle Owen!" Aiden scampered over to him, and the others followed, surrounding him like a litter of puppies anticipating a treat. Owen smiled at Lena over their heads and then set about pouring the cider.

"Is that a snow fort?" he asked as the kids gulped the warm drink. "Those walls look good and solid."

"Me and Mom made it!" Sam shouted happily. Lena's heart skipped a beat, expanded and contracted as she watched a series of emotions pass over Sam's face in just a few seconds. Joy and pride gave way to shock the moment that he realized what he just said, and she watched guilt and embarrassment follow close behind.

It doesn't mean anything, she told herself. *Every kid slips up and calls their teacher Mom sometimes. It's like that. Don't make a big thing out of it, not even in your own head.*

Owen, bless him, didn't react at all. His expression didn't even shift. He just set the empty thermos aside and asked, "Can I help you build up these walls?"

Sam's expression was unreadable now, and it took him a moment to respond. But then he nodded and trudged back over to the fort, hand in hand with Owen. The other kids followed, eager to help, and soon they were all working on the fort together. Once the walls, complete with an arched doorway and windows, were as high as Sam's head, the kids started to lose interest. Zoe flopped theatrically backwards into the snow, and Aiden picked up one of the saucers.

"Anyone want to race?"

Zoe popped up. "I do!"

"Slackers," Liam muttered under his breath, still working away at a snow couch he had designed.

Sam was still and quiet, looking at the sled that Owen had given him. He still hadn't worked up the courage to ride it himself yet. But now, without saying a word, he grabbed the sled and marched up the hill after Aiden and Zoe. They waited for him at the top, cheered him on as he climbed aboard his sled, and all started down the hill with a cry of "Three! Two! One! Go!"

Sam managed his sled perfectly, leaving the bigger kids in the dust. The spectators cheered him on from the sidelines, Lena so loudly that it made her throat ache.

Sam waved at them, his smile visible even from across the yard, and went racing back up the hill. He accomplished several more perfect runs while Lena stood watching. Her nose was numb, but she didn't care. She could watch him forever.

"I don't think they'll hold out much longer," Owen said as they watched Sam trudge up the hill for the umpteenth time. The sun was sinking behind the trees, taking with it what little warmth the day had offered. Owen kissed Lena's frozen cheek and said, "I'm going to go in and make some hot cocoa."

"Sounds good," Lena said without taking her eyes off of Sam. "Thanks."

Zoe and Aiden raced down the hill before Sam reached the peak. When he finally got there and started off, his sled veered too far to the left. Lena watched with growing horror as he drifted closer to the trees, but there was nothing that she could do from here.

Then the sled hit a patch of ice. It careened into a sapling, and Sam went flying. Heart hammering in her chest, Lena sprinted toward him, in motion before he had even hit the ground.

He lay still where he had fallen, and Lena felt a panic like nothing she had ever experienced before. She had nearly reached him when her foot landed on a hidden patch of ice, maybe the same patch that had sent Sam flying. She pinwheeled her arms, trying to keep her balance, but her feet flew out from under her, and she landed in a heap in the snow.

At some point in her panic she'd lost her hat, and her crazy curls tumbled in front of her eyes. When she pushed herself up and brushed the hair away with snow-dusted gloves, Sam was sitting up. He was looking at her, tears in his eyes, blood on his lip... and he was *laughing*. He tried to catch his breath to speak, but he couldn't get the words out. Just collapsed back into laughter, whirling his arms in a pantomime of Lena's attempts to keep her balance, and she started laughing too.

The other kids came running, their boots crunching through the snow.

"Careful of the ice," Lena cautioned, still sprawled in the snow. She crawled over to Sam and wiped the blood off of his lip with one gloved finger. He let out one last little laugh and leaned into her, throwing his arms around her in a fierce hug.

"Are you okay?" Zoe shouted at a volume more suited to a football field than the five or so feet that currently separated them.

"I'm okay," Lena said. She looked down at Sam. "Are you okay?"

"Yeah, I'm okay." His arms were still around her, and she kissed the top of his snow-damp hair. Where had *his* hat gone? She looked around halfheartedly, not really caring enough to search for it.

"Are you ready for some hot cocoa?" she asked. "Or do you want to stay outside a while longer?"

"Hot cocoa, please."

Zoe and Aiden started up a chant of "Hot cocoa! Hot cocoa!" as they raced toward the house. Lena pushed herself to her feet and then helped Sam up. They followed the other kids, and Sam left his mittened hand in hers as they walked. She managed to scoop up both of their hats on the way back to the house, all without letting go.

Such was life, Lena reflected as they made their way through the snow. You fell—sometimes you bled—but you dusted the snow off, and you kept moving. Highs and lows. But the highs of having children in her life were so high that the lows were worth it.

This was going to be the best Christmas ever.

21

FALLYN

FALLYN SHIVERED VIOLENTLY under David's thick jacket, which she was using as a makeshift blanket, but didn't turn her binoculars away from the window of Graham's house. Luckily, they'd convinced Alicia her presence would do more harm than good, and only the two of them had holed up in the tiny rental car for almost four hours now. The wealthy man's down-the-street neighbors were apparently not home, so Fallyn and Shaw had decided to borrow their snow-covered driveway until or unless they were told otherwise. They had an excuse about being lost along with a wrinkled map at the ready just in case they came home.

"There," she whispered. Graham's form appeared in the window once again, moving toward the door, and a wave of disappointment ran through Fallyn when he didn't come through it.

She cursed softly as another shiver ran through her, and she couldn't bring herself to protest when she heard Shaw putting the keys in and starting the car up once again. They had little way of knowing exactly when the kidnapper would contact Graham, only that it would be today, and they'd still need enough gas to follow him once he finally decided to leave the house. When she'd agreed to this job, an hours-long stake-out outside of the victim's father's house had been the last thing she would've expected, but it seemed like the only option they had left.

Shaw's hand rubbed at her shoulder, and she relaxed into it, letting out a sigh.

"Want to eat our sandwiches now?" she asked, reaching in front of her seat to grab the bag they'd packed with the things. It was starting to warm up already, and she gave silent thanks to the brand new car's heating system as she reached into the bag and pulled out her sandwich. It might be a late lunch, but at least they could eat it in relative comfort.

"At least we know we didn't miss him," Shaw said, accepting his PB&J.

"We knew it might take a while," Fallyn agreed, taking her first bite. Ellie's tangy strawberry jelly cut the richness of the peanut butter perfectly, and she felt some semblance of relief as she chewed. She reached for her mug and washed it down with a swig of coffee, pleased that it was still quite warm.

"It was about an hour ago when Maura left," Shaw said. "It'd make some sense to have her out of the house when he goes. I doubt he wants anyone trying to tag along with him when he goes to make the pickup. My bet is that he leaves before she gets back."

"I guess we'll see," Fallyn said, but her hopes weren't high. She was too cold for high hopes at this point.

David's hand went back to her shoulder, and he rubbed it

softly before saying, "Sorry, but I think we should probably shut the car off again."

Fallyn nodded slowly, knowing he was right and holding in a tired sigh. The cold ache in her back and legs told her she was getting too old for stuff like this.

"No problem," she said, taking another bite of her sandwich as the engine quieted.

She looked over to grab her coffee mug for another sip, but Shaw jabbed his finger back toward the door, and she whirled.

"Is it—?"

It was. Graham Hazelton strode out of the house, and she could see the tension in his gait through the powerful binoculars. He fidgeted nervously, shaking his head as he marched through the snow toward his car.

Fallyn let the binoculars drop, sighing with relief as she shoved the last of her sandwich into her mouth. Their wait was over. Shaw put the keys in the ignition but kept the car off until Graham pulled out of his driveway.

Once he did, Shaw let him get a solid thirty seconds ahead before pulling out behind him. The drive was slow but difficult, with winding roads, some unplowed, that left Graham obscured for minutes at a time that had her nerves jangling. They had almost lost him on several occasions, and she was just starting to stress about gas when they reached a long gravelly road nearly an hour away. Snow-covered trees flanked them on all sides, and Shaw let the other man get an even larger lead on them. They hadn't seen another car in miles, and they'd stick out like a sore thumb if he noticed them.

As they crested a steep hill, a rush of panic ran through

Fallyn. Graham had disappeared completely. Her eyes flitted from side to side, but he was nowhere to be seen. David cursed. "Maybe he clocked us and pulled off somewhere."

Fallyn fidgeted nervously, continuing her search, but felt a rush of relief as she noticed the beginnings of a driveway cutting through the wooded area just ahead on their right. "There," she said, jabbing her finger toward it.

Shaw pulled close but turned off his headlights and put it in park.

"We're on foot from here," he said.

Fallyn nodded silently, grabbing her audio recorder and taking a final pull from her coffee mug before opening the car door. The critical moment was finally here, and, strangely, she felt a calmness settle over her at the thought. They'd faced worse than this when they were working the Emily Addison case; they could handle this too.

"Let's use these trees for cover," Fallyn said, leading the way down the tree line that flanked the driveway. It was a long, winding stretch, with only one set of tire tracks. She let out a sigh of relief. That meant she was right; Ivan was likely long gone. Graham's car came into view before long. Fallyn used her binoculars to confirm that he was no longer in it, then crept closer.

Twigs snapped, and snow crunched under Shaw's feet behind her, but they were in little danger of being heard at this distance, assuming he was actually inside. A light flicked on, clearly visible in the waning sunlight, confirming that he was, and she put up her index finger. "Let's get a closer look," she whispered.

They trudged slowly toward one of the windows, staying out of view. She stopped when she was about a dozen feet away, pulling out her binoculars, and got a clear view of him as he stepped back into the room, which appeared to be a kitchen, shaking his head nervously. He turned toward the one closed door, pulling it open and flicking on the light, then appeared to begin descending a set of stairs.

He returned less than a minute later, shutting the door behind him before collapsing against it, hand going to his eyes as if wiping away tears. He sat there for a long moment before collecting himself, his chest heaving as he let out several deep breaths. Pushing himself to a standing position, he reached for his pocket and pulled out his phone.

Fallyn's heart thumped audibly in her chest, and a panic colder than the chill air ran through her veins.

Was the little girl dead? Was she not there as agreed upon? She'd been so sure she'd figured it all out...what if she was wrong and not telling the police had cost Wren Hazelton her life?

Fallyn swallowed the rush of bile that rose to her throat as she watched Graham pacing the living room floor, cell phone to her ear.

"I'm going inside," she whispered. "I want to see if I can hear what he's saying."

Shaw shook his head vigorously, "Not an option. I—"

"He isn't violent," Fallyn interjected.

"A lot of people aren't until they're backed into a corner. If your hunch is right, he has a *lot* to lose, Fallyn. You wait here and I'll go instead."

Fallyn shook her head, thinking back to their walk up here. "You'll be like a bull in a china shop. I'm smaller and quieter. It has to be me. You know that, Shaw."

He met her gaze for a long moment, then nodded almost imperceptibly.

"Take this." He pulled at the corner of her jacket, shoving a can of pepper spray into her pocket. "I'll be watching, and I'll have 911 cued up and ready. If I have any sense at all that you're in danger, I'm pressing the button and then coming in."

She nodded, handing him the binoculars and leaning in for a quick kiss before darting toward the house.

She moved on silent feet around back, stopping at the door. It squeaked almost imperceptibly, and she waited for a few seconds, on high alert. She could hear Graham's voice coming from the other room, so she stepped inside, heart hammering. On her tiptoes, she made her way to the door leading from the kitchen to the living room and pressed her ear against it.

"—want the scoop on the Wren Hazelton case, get to 22 Hunter's Circle ASAP," he was muttering in a strange, guttural tone.

Was he calling the police?

He went silent for a long moment, then began speaking again, starting the conversation anew. "Hi, is this WRSQ news?"

She had to bite back a snarl of rage. He wasn't calling for help. He was staging a press conference.

Fallyn re-centered herself, backing away from the door. She crept back out the way she came, focused on one thing and one thing only: finding out if Wren Hazelton was alive and well in the house somewhere.

She would deal with the girl's father later.

With only the light of the moon shimmering off the snow

to guide her, she crept around the perimeter of the house, looking for some way to see inside—

A jolt of excitement shot through her as she caught sight of a half window, nearly obscured by the snow.

Ignoring the cold, she dropped down to her belly and pressed her face against the dirty glass. For a long moment, she searched what looked like an empty room. Then she saw it. A little futon tucked in the corner. On it, the motionless body of a little girl with tangled strawberry blond curls.

Please, God, don't let her be—

At that moment, Wren rolled onto her side and Fallyn went dizzy with relief. She was alive. Wren was alive. Fallyn pushed herself to standing, when she felt a cold, hard object press against her cheek.

Click.

"Make a sound and I shoot," Graham said, his voice quiet and deadly. "Turn around, nice and slow," he continued.

Fallyn nodded slowly, eyeing the pistol. This wasn't the first time she'd had one pointed at her, but the familiarity hadn't made it any less terrifying.

"Move."

He gripped her arm and led her back toward the door, his gun trained on her the whole time.

"Where's your partner?"

She swallowed hard as Graham moved around her until they were face to face, just a few yards apart.

"We got a bead on Ivan's location. Shaw is trying to run him down before he reaches the border," Fallyn managed through her chattering teeth.

Graham nodded, glancing out the window. "Good."

Fallyn swallowed, saying nothing as Graham began to

pace back and forth, breathing erratically and gesturing with the weapon as he muttered quietly to himself. Her life was entirely in the hands of a desperate man who had nothing to lose.

"Why did you have to come here?" he asked, shaking his head bitterly. "It was done. Just another hour or two and–"

"You would've gotten away with it?" she cut in, doing everything she could to keep his attention away from the hand she was slowly inching toward her pocket.

He shook his head, looking toward the ceiling as her fingers closed over the canister of pepper spray. Almost instantly, she disregarded the idea. A pepper-sprayed man with a gun still posed a major threat. Instead, she pressed the button on the recording device she'd brought with her.

"I saw your face when you found out about the blood and thought it was Wren's. You looked gutted. I know you'd never have chosen for things to end up this way. It went all wrong, and you couldn't figure out how to stop it."

"How did you figure it out?" he asked, his tone calm when he looked back toward her.

"We saw the ransom note on your desk, and a Samaritan identified Ivan from the video taken at the mechanic's shop. I put two and two together."

He chuckled softly. "That double-crossing bastard. Serves him right. And to think I let *him*, of all people, get one over on me like this."

"He betrayed you," she began. "If things went the way you planned, it would've all been fine. He could've taken his payment as agreed upon, but he got greedy."

"It was just supposed to be some good publicity...swing public opinion my way after that embarrassing debacle a couple months back," he whispered. "No *real* harm was supposed to come to anyone, least of all my kid."

"I know that, Graham." She had to stall a little longer for David to make his move. "We can still salvage this situation, though. You can still get that moment you were looking for," she said, barely suppressing a wince as she heard a faint rustling outside. "When the press comes, you—"

Graham's eyes went flat with fury as he closed the gap between them in an instant. "You lying witch. You aren't alone," he grunted, pinning her arms to her side easily. She flailed wildly, but it was no use. Within seconds, her back was pressed against his chest, his pistol at her temple.

"You don't have to do this," she whispered, not daring to continue her struggle.

"You know too much," Graham said, and Fallyn could hear the shaking fear and anxiety in his tone. This was a man on the edge. He continued blabbering, seemingly more to himself than anyone else. "I'll lose my career, my freedom, my family. I can't afford to go to prison. They'll chew me up and spit me out."

"Okay, so run, then. I'll give you my keys, you walk me to your car with the gun trained on me, and then just drive off. Take our phones with you. We'll have no way of going after you then."

"And then what?" Graham said, laughing humorlessly. "Live the rest of my life as a fugitive?"

Fallyn searched desperately for the right words. "All I wanted was to get the little girl back to her mother. I'm not a cop, Graham."

"You're just a lying *snake*," Graham spat. "Nothing but lies and deceit since you got here. I think a better idea might be to kill you and that partner of yours. I might even be able to make it look like a mistake. A tragic accident when I ran into the nosy detectives I thought were my daughter's kidnappers."

There was a crash, and Shaw burst through the door. A jolt of surprise ran through Fallyn as she saw Alicia striding in just behind him.

"What the hell?" Graham barked. "Leesh, what—"

"Let her go," David grunted, but he stopped in his tracks as Graham pressed the tip of his gun farther into the side of Fallyn's head.

"This isn't you, Graham," Alicia said softly, holding out her open palm. "So far, no one has been hurt, and you should want to keep it that way."

"And why should I?" he spat, his breath hot on Fallyn's shoulders. "You all came here intending to get me locked up, so what do I care?"

"Think of our daughter, Graham. How do you want her to see you after all this is said and done? Are you going to kill me, too? What's your plan for the future?"

Graham's grip softened slightly. "I—If I do this your way, I *have* no future."

"You still *can* have a future if you come clean and do your time," Alicia continued. "And your daughter can too. Don't let it be marred by something this horrible."

"Daddy?"

Graham's grip on Fallyn's shoulder loosened even further, but the gun stayed pressed to her temple. "Go back downstairs, sweetie," he said softly. "We're discussing something right now, but we'll be down to get you in a minute."

"Why are you holding her like that?" Wren demanded, looking sleepy-faced and confused. She went silent for a second, then Fallyn heard the pitter-patter of her footsteps followed by a gasp as she sprinted out from behind them, making a beeline for her mother.

"Mommy!"

The man behind her let out a sob, and the pressure on Fallyn's temple suddenly gave way as Graham shoved her forward.

"I'm sorry. God, I'm so, so sorry," he whispered, setting the gun on the floor beside him before collapsing to his knees.

Shaw closed the gap in an instant, grabbing the pistol and unloading it before stuffing it into his pocket. He clenched his fists, and Fallyn could see the rage burning in his eyes as he eyed Graham, but he strode back toward Alicia and her daughter.

"Is she alright?"

"Yup. I'm okay." Wren's curls bounced wildly as she nodded, seemingly oblivious to the life and death situation that they'd just been in. "No booboos. I bit that man on time, though. Hard."

Fallyn let out a short laugh but kept her eyes trained on Graham. Graham Hazelton was egocentric, brash, and a jerk, but he wasn't a murderer. And somehow, despite all that had happened, she found herself hoping that maybe one day he could change. One day, he could redeem himself.

Not for his sake, but for Wren's.

Birdie's.

Fallyn's thoughts scattered as Shaw pulled her into an embrace. She relaxed into his arms, a deep sense of relief settling over her. "We did it," she said, just barely able to make out the sound of sirens in the distance. "We really did it."

He pulled back slightly, then peppered her face with near-frantic kisses.

"*You* did it. And you took ten years off my life in the process." He guided her toward the floor, and they sat together, watching the joyous reunion between Wren and her mother.

It was priceless.

22

ANDREA

Wyatt was due to arrive any minute, and Andrea had a full assembly line set up in the kitchen. He was taking Jeffrey on a ski trip that wasn't costing Andrea a thing. Wyatt had a guest pass that came with his yearly membership, and he had offered to bring Jeffrey along. Between that and everything else the marvelous young man had done for their family, well... a portable feast was the least that she could do.

Most of the food that she had made for their weekend away was already packed in a cooler. Now she just needed to pack up the food she had made for the drive. Andrea's nerves buzzed with anxiety as she ladled generous portions of beef stew into travel thermoses. She glanced at the cuckoo clock on the kitchen wall that had belonged to her dad, and her stomach sank. She knew that she should be grateful to Wyatt for taking Jeffrey on such a fun weekend trip—and she was, really she was—but a large part of her was dreading it. She didn't want to stand in her driveway and watch them drive off. It felt like another nightmare waiting to happen. Sending Jeffrey into the mountains without her felt like more than her overwrought nerves could take.

It wasn't snowing yet, but it would be soon. With luck, they would already be safe inside the lodge when the first flakes started to fall. She trusted Wyatt as much as she had ever trusted anyone... but she had trusted her dad completely, and she had lost him. She had almost lost Jeffrey. Horrible things could happen to the best people. And even though Jeffrey was far safer on the slopes with Wyatt than he would be with Andrea, a huge part of her wanted to follow them up there. Not because she thought that she could protect them from natural disasters, but because at least then she would *know*. She wouldn't have to sit at home worrying about Wyatt driving through the snow, Jeffrey being swept up in an avalanche or falling and cracking his skull skiing or getting separated from Wyatt in a snowstorm and lost again in the wilderness.

"Stop." Andrea surprised herself by speaking out loud, a knee-jerk response to the uncontrolled turmoil of her thoughts. She took a long, deep breath as she screwed the tops on to the thermoses full of beef stew.

This is all part of working through trauma, Andrea reminded herself as she packed up a dozen toffee chip cookies. They were still warm from the oven, and she took a big bite out of one before tucking the rest of them into Jeffrey's lunch bag. *Old fears get bigger. New fears crop up. You can't stop that from happening. But you can choose not to let those fears control you.*

The anxiety that had plagued her since Jeffrey's ordeal in the mountains felt crippling at times. Sometimes she missed her dad so much that she could hardly breathe. She couldn't control the fears that plagued her or the grief that weighed her down, but she could choose how she responded to them. She could acknowledge her fear, respect it as a deep desire to keep her son safe... and then push right on past it.

Andrea loved her son too much to wind him up in bubble wrap and set him in front of a screen all winter. She wasn't going to keep her nature-loving son in a bubble. Despite the fear that plagued her, she was so proud of him. She loved his passion for building shelters in the woods, and she was in awe of how well he had recovered from the trauma he had endured in the mountains.

Wyatt had saved Jeffrey in more ways than one, and he wasn't going to let anything happen to him now.

Andrea loved her son enough to let him go—albeit with lots of food, enough clothes for a full week away, and a wilderness survival cell phone she'd purchased for him but let him go nonetheless. And then she had to remember to count her blessings.

It was nearly Christmas. The knowledge that little Wren Hazelton was home for the holidays was a huge weight off her heart. Andrea's place was decked out in old heirlooms with warm strings of lights across the top of nearly every wall in the house. Their first Christmas without her dad would be painful, but they would get through. Cherry Blossom Point had welcomed them with open arms, and Andrea was deeply grateful for the community they had found there.

Her mom had been ready to toss the old outdoor lights that Dad had strung up every year, so Andrea had saved them and put them up at her new place. More accurately, Cole had strung them up on every side of the little house while Andrea shouted directions from ground level. Her grumpy mechanic was thawing by the day, even as the weather outside grew increasingly frigid. Even now, she could hear him and Jeffrey laughing and joking over a video game.

For their first date, Cole had taken Andrea to the nicest restaurant around. The fancy French place two towns over had a waiting list a mile long, but the owner had owed Cole a favor ever since the mechanic had saved his classic car from the chop shop. The date had started out a bit awkward, with stilted conversation on Andrea's side and long silences on Cole's. They had regarded the ornate menus in silence for a long minute... and then Andrea had set the menu down, smiled across the table at Cole, and said that she'd just as soon skip the escargot and head to Gayle's for a fat, juicy lamb burger.

The warm relief on Cole's face washed any lingering awkwardness away, and they'd made their escape giggling like a couple of high school kids playing hooky. At Hunters Gathering, they'd scored a seat by the fire and eaten their burgers in easy silence, then lingered for hours over fries and cider, talking about everything.

It had been about two weeks since that first date, and they had seen each other nearly every day. Cole wasn't the type of guy to show up with hothouse flowers or boxes of chocolate, but he *had* come to her house and put snow tires on when there was a storm headed their way. He had driven over at six in the morning to give her a jump start after she had left her lights on all night. And when she'd asked him if he wanted to come with her to a Christmas tree lot, he had driven her into the woods in his brother's truck and cut down her chosen tree himself.

Just as Andrea put the last containers into Jeffrey's bag—

two thermoses of hot apple cider—the doorbell rang. Jeffrey's footsteps thundered across the hardwood floor as he ran to answer the door. An unwelcome jolt of adrenaline shot through Andrea's body, and she took a moment to steady herself. When she felt sure that she could greet Wyatt with a warm smile instead of a pained grimace, she walked out to the living room.

"Sounds like you've been spending a lot of time around here," Wyatt was saying to Cole, his tone guarded. Was he feeling protective? That was so sweet, but it was like watching a rangy puppy trying to frighten a wolfhound. Andrea had to bite back a laugh. Cole's expression was blank, but when he looked at her, she saw a warm glint of amusement in his eyes.

"It's good to meet the young man that Jeff and Andrea speak so highly of," Cole said when he turned back to Wyatt. He offered his hand, and Wyatt shook it. "Where are you two headed this weekend?"

"Sugarloaf." Wyatt relaxed a bit, smiling in anticipation of the slopes.

"My favorite spot," Cole approved.

"You ski?"

"Born and raised in Maine. 'Course I ski. Been years since I made it to Sugarloaf, though." Cole put an arm around Andrea's shoulders and added, "Maybe we'll join you next time."

"Sounds good." Wyatt turned his attention to Jeffrey. "Ready to go?"

"Yep!" Jeffrey grabbed his duffel bag off of the floor and slung it over his shoulder.

"Where's your coat?" Andrea asked. Cole ran a light hand down her back as he moved away.

"It's in the bag."

"It's cold outside."

Jeffrey gave her a long-suffering look and plucked at his wool sweater. "We're just going from here to the car."

"You packed your toothbrush?"

"Yes, Mom."

"And clean underwear?"

"*Mom!*" Jeffrey gave her a beleaguered look. "I packed everything!"

"Worst case scenario," Wyatt said, "there's shops up there. It's not like we're going into the wilderness."

"I packed everything," he repeated petulantly.

"Headed out?" Cole asked. He was carrying the cooler full of food and the warm meal that Andrea had packed in Jeffrey's school lunchbox.

"Yep," Wyatt said. "We should hit the road and make sure we beat the storm. It isn't supposed to snow until close to midnight, but I want to give us plenty of extra time."

"Wise man. Let me help you out to the car."

Jeffrey shoved his feet into his boots and raced out the door ahead of Wyatt, who opened up the back of his truck so that they could put everything inside.

"Don't forget to brush your teeth," Andrea said weakly.

"Okay, Mom." Jeffrey wrapped his arms around her in a real, solid hug. She held him tightly for a long moment before letting go.

Cole reached out and ruffled Jeffrey's hair. "Have a great time, kid."

"You have a hat?" Andrea asked as Jeffrey climbed up into the truck.

"I have *two*," he said with a grin.

"Let's get going!" Wyatt closed Jeffrey's door and then gave Andrea a quick, one-armed hug. "I'll give you a call when we get there, and I'll send some pictures of him on the slopes."

"Thank you." Andrea pulled Wyatt in for a real hug, holding him as tightly as she'd held her son. "For everything."

Wyatt smiled and shrugged, but there was a shakiness to his attempt at nonchalance. "I never got to meet my brother. I like spending time with Jeffrey." He trotted around to the other side of the truck and gave them one last wave, and then they were off.

Andrea stood and watched them go. Cole put an arm around her waist, and she leaned into him.

"You gonna be okay?" he asked.

"Yeah. I will. I'm just feeling nervous."

"It'll take them a few hours to get there. How about a distraction?"

Andrea smiled up at him. "What did you have in mind?"

"Movie theater? Some fantasy epic or silly Christmas movie?"

"And a big bucket of popcorn," Andrea agreed. "Sounds great."

If she sat around the house, she would be checking her phone obsessively. Even now, she was staring after Wyatt's truck like she could keep them safe through sheer force of will. If they went to a movie now, she could get her mind off of it and check her phone right around the time that Jeffrey and Wyatt were due to arrive at the lodge.

When she finally tore her eyes away from the bend in the road where Wyatt's truck had driven out of sight, she noticed that Cole had driven his brother's truck over that day. It was parked across the street, a looming reminder of the family that wouldn't be there to feast with them or exchange gifts this Christmas... or any other.

"This time of year is hard," she said quietly, wrapping her arms around Cole's waist. He followed her gaze and gave his brother's truck a long look before looking back down at her. "Are you okay?"

"Not having my brother here will always feel like a missing limb," he murmured in a low voice. "But this year?" He kissed her forehead. "Yeah. I'm okay. Let's get you that bucket of popcorn."

Cole released his hold on her as they crossed the street, and he headed for the passenger side.

"What are you doing?" she asked, pausing by the front of the truck.

Cole turned to her with a gentle smile. "Why don't you drive this time?"

Andrea froze for a second, fully aware of what an honor that was. Cole didn't let *anyone* drive his brother's truck.

Except, apparently, for her.

"Sure," she said, the tone of her voice belying the casual response. She climbed up into the driver's seat, and Cole handed her the keys. He touched his fingers to the old wooden rosary hanging from the rearview mirror as Andrea started the car. As she drove slowly down the road, Cole turned on the radio. Quiet Christmas music filled the cab, sung with a country twang.

Andrea reached out for Cole's hand, and he squeezed her

fingers gently. She was filled with a sudden gratitude that eclipsed the grief and the fear that she carried with her every day. Life was bumpy and hard sometimes, but she was so grateful that they had found each other.

This first Christmas without her dad was going to hurt. But they would get through it.

And after that?

She shot Cole a glance.

The New Year was looking just a little brighter.

Pick up the next and final book in the Cherry Blossom Point series, From Start to Finish, and dive into Alicia Hazelton's story!

Looking for more women's fiction books by Christine Gael? Check out Maeve's Girls...

La Pierre, Louisiana had never seen anything like Maeve Blanchard, and they never will again. After 75 years, five husbands, four daughters, and one bootleg whiskey ring, Maeve has finally been called home to be with the Lord...or with someone, somewhere, at any rate.

But while Maeve took her impending demise in stride, her four girls have had their worlds turned upside down.

There's 54 year-old Lena, Maeve's love-child who left home at sixteen to get away from the stain of her mother's wild life and never looked back. Kate, who married far too young and lost herself somewhere along the way. Sasha, who has followed in her mother's high-heeled footsteps and is forced to come face to face with the demons from her past. And Maggie, Maeve's niece who she raised as her own.

Despite the complex relationships they shared with their mother in life, Maeve's girls each need to make their peace with her in death, and they're finally ready to come home to La Pierre to do it. The only question now is whether La Pierre is ready for them...

For readers of Liane Moriarty (Big Little Lies), Danielle Steele, Sandra Brown, Iris Johansen, Debbie Macomber, and Fern Michaels.

ONE

If you're reading this, that means I've gone to the big casino in the sky. And frankly, I'm not sorry. Especially if it's hurricane season.

I know some of y'all aren't going to be happy about being back in La Pierre (especially you, Lena, bless your heart). But I have faith in your ability to survive most anything, for a time. It's a trait you girls share with your mama...and cockroaches, ha! But it's also a trait that has served me very well. And, now that you've each had a chance to get a little more living under your belts, I hope you'll realize that it's served you well, too.

What comes next will probably seem like a punishment to at least two out of the four of you, but time is short, and I can't be fussed to write out the whole thought process behind my decision with the little I have left. For now, I hope you'll trust that this wasn't some random scheme I cooked up just to get on your nerves one last time.

For starters, as you know by now, I've advised Alistair that y'all need to come home for the reading of this will. There will be no disbursement of funds or property until or unless that happens. I've already told him that calling in on some newfangled video program like MyFace, or some intercom doo-hickey, doesn't count. I want all four of you, same room, no exceptions (unless one of you has beaten me to the grave after the writing of this letter, something I pray to any god that has a mind to hear me won't be the case). If you're listening to this, though, that means you've all done what you were told for once, and I've already achieved in death what I couldn't in life. Somebody get the holy water, it's a miracle! But that also means each of you is struggling right now. Whether it's because I'm gone, or because you're here in La Pierre, try to be kind and patient with each other. It's going to be a long three months.

'Why?' you ask?

Because that's how long the four of you will need to live in Blanchard Manor before the deed and ownership of everything inside it will be transferred into your names. What you do with it after that is none of my concern. Sell it. Raze it. Make it into a hippy commune or a taco stand. I don't care. Beyond that, I ask of you the following:

Check on Harold for me. He's not the same since Annalise passed and he needs looking after.

Be careful with the jewelry. Lord knows, I love it gaudy, but some of it looks fake even though it isn't. Whatever you do, though, don't get it appraised down at Elsie's Gems and Antiquities. (Sorry, Alistair, I know she's your sister-in-law, but we both know she'd rob a blind man of his cane if she had the chance. Plus, she's never gotten over me winning that blue ribbon with the pecan pie I picked up at the Piggly Wiggly back in seventy-nine.)

And, last but not least, when clearing out the house, start from the attic and work your way down. That seems to be the order of things, doesn't it? The dusty old memories at the top, down to the stuff we use every day in our living spaces. But I'm also hoping that you'll come to view me a little less harshly if you start at the beginning. If you still feel the same way about me in three months as you do now? Well, that's all right, too. At the end of the day, closure is what I'm looking for here. Both for you girls and for me, too. Even if that means some of y'all closing the door and never looking back again.

Most of all, know this...

I did the best I could with what I had at the time, and gave you all the love I had to spare.

XOXO

-Maeve

TWO

Alistair Raynaud, Attorney at Law, slipped off his glasses and cleared his throat as he laid the swath of papers on his desk. "I'm afraid that's all, for right now."

Lena wasn't surprised to see the sheen of tears in his tired eyes. Alistair and her mother had known each other for nearly seven decades, and he'd been on retainer since the

Nixon era. He'd handled all of the details of Maeve's annulment, both late in life divorces, and the untimely death of two spouses, making sure her interests were always looked after. He'd also kept her out of the slammer more times than any of them could count.

By Lena's estimation, Alistair was probably weeping for the loss of his best client as much as he was at having to say goodbye to a friend.

From her vantage point directly behind her sisters, Lena could see Sasha's tanned, bare shoulders shaking, and Kate as she dabbed at her own cheeks with a handkerchief, while Maggie's soft sobs filled the otherwise silent room.

But Lena's eyes were dry as a bone.

Maeve was dead right when she'd assumed that her eldest daughter would rather chew off her own leg than be back in the bear trap that was her hometown of La Pierre, Louisiana. In fact, Lena would've given up her entire inheritance to be anywhere else right now...

On that note, she stood and slid the strap of her purse over her shoulder, her legs surprisingly shaky.

"Look, I know my sisters are going through a tough time, and I don't want to add to that, so I'm going to make this quick and to the point. I don't want it," she said firmly. "I don't want any of it," Lena repeated for good measure, shooting a stiff smile at Alistair. "If you can just write up a release of some kind that I can sign in order to hand my share over to my sisters, I'll be on my way. I'm happy to pay you for your time."

She spared a quick glance at her watch and winced. Her flight back to Seattle didn't leave for another ten hours, which meant she had a good seven to spare. She made a mental note to check the movie times at the cinema near the airport. A double feature with a large popcorn there, followed by a double scotch and soda at the airport, and just maybe she'd get rid of the bad taste in her mouth.

She looked up to find Sasha staring at her over her shoulder, wide cornflower eyes full of resentment. "Are you serious right now? Mama is dead, and you're going to breeze in and breeze out in less than twenty-four hours like it's nothing?"

Lena resisted the urge to turn on her sensible heels and walk. This was one of the seven hundred reasons she hadn't wanted to come back here. The drama. Everything Maeve-related fairly oozed with it. Get too close, it'd rub off on a body and cling, like the sticky underside of a garden snail on a cobblestone pathway.

Worse, though? Once it was on you, there was no way to ever truly get it off. Nobody knew that better than Lena.

She took a steadying breath and met Sasha's accusing gaze, once again momentarily taken aback by how much she favored Maeve. Ten years younger than Lena, at 44, Sasha could've easily passed for 39 and, if Lena were to guess, probably did whenever possible. Her face was heart-shaped, like their mother's, only slightly more round, which gave her an air of innocence. Her almost preternaturally blue eyes tilted up at the corners just a little, and glinted with mischief, as if to say, *"Dare me"*. The contrasting effect was lethal. Men desired her almost as much as other women despised her.

Dolly may have pled for the mercy of an intoxicating temptress named Jolene, but she might as well have been singing to Sasha. That apple had fallen directly in front of the tree that was Maeve. Maybe that was why Lena couldn't hold her sister's gaze for very long without looking away...

She shoved those thoughts aside and tried to keep her tone even and calm as she tried again. "Having me here is only going to make things worse for you three," she reasoned. "I'm not good at pretending. Never have been. You all know it," she added, sparing a glance at her other two sisters, who had turned and now looked on in silence. "Why do that to yourselves?"

Or me.

"Ah, actually," Alistair said, his voice cutting through the tension vibrating like a live wire between them, "I'm afraid that isn't really an option anyway, Lena."

Her pulse skittered as she turned her attention to the old man behind the desk.

"What does that mean?" she demanded in a low voice.

Alistair shifted his considerable girth in the chair, making it squeal in protest, before reaching for a second, unopened envelope on his desk.

He held it up with a wry smile. "For what it's worth, I advised her against this, girls..."

Lena instantly bristled at the way he addressed them— even her youngest sister was over forty, for crying out loud— but her irritation fizzled away as she read the words scrawled across the front of the envelope in her mother's no-nonsense handwriting.

Part deux, to read when Lena tries to walk out...

. . .

Ah, Maeve, you wily old so and so. Lena let out a breath, shoulders going ramrod straight. Amazing that her mother was no longer of this earth and still found a way to get under her skin so completely.

She inclined her head but refused to retake her seat. "Get on with it, then."

Alistair tore open the envelope and perched his glasses on the end of his nose before beginning to read.

Should any of my children leave town before the three months is up, or forfeit their share, my entire estate will go to the La Pierre Improvement and Beautification Committee, in honor of the city I loved so dearly. The estate will be split four ways, or not at all.

Meaning, if she left before the three months was up, not only would her sisters be left with nothing, but the town that had been an albatross around her neck since the day she was born would get a three-quarter of a million dollar makeover. Because, apparently, Maeve had decided that a right hook was always better when followed by a bone-jarring uppercut.

Lena pinched her eyes closed and shook her head slowly, a low laugh escaping her lips.

Well played, Mother.

Diabolical? Yup. Manipulative? Definitely. Risky? Always. But in life, as in death, Maeve Blanchard had never been stupid. She'd known exactly what she was doing.

Lena didn't wait to hear more as she forced her feet into motion.

"Where are you going?" Sasha demanded, her voice shrill.

"Lena, at least listen to what else Alistair has to say," Maggie added.

But it was Kate's words that stayed with her long after the door closed behind her.

"Leave her be. She won't go far. She just needs some time to get her head straight."

~

"Double scotch and soda with a twist, please."

Lena settled onto the barstool with a groan and kept her eyes cast down as the bartender shuffled off to make her drink. It had been years since she'd shown her face in La Pierre. Prior to that short visit, it had been almost a decade. Surely no one would recognize her. She looked nothing like the brash young woman who'd left town at age sixteen as if the hounds of hell were nipping at her heels. She'd made damn sure of it.

"You're one of Maeve's girls, aren't you?"

Less than two minutes, and the jig was already up. Swallowing a sigh, she turned to find a man in his late sixties seated at the short section of the L-shaped bar, eying her with something akin to pity. The only question was, did he feel sorry for her because her mother had died, or because Maeve had been her mother at all? Both would check out.

"I am, yes," she acknowledged with a nod. "Lena."

He squinted, scratching at one bushy eyebrow with a greasy fingernail as he studied her. "One of Vinnie's daughters?"

"Nope. That would be my sisters, Kate and Sasha."

The bartender returned with Lena's drink and set it on the bar before hitching a hip against a cooler filled with frosty beer mugs.

"Claire's daughter, then? That was a dang shame, her passing so young. Car accident, yeah?"

"Actually, that's my sister, Maggie. Maeve adopted her when my Aunt Claire died in the wreck."

This was what happened when your family tree was more like a tawdry tangle of gnarled branches than it was a mighty oak or a proud sequoia. People asked questions... made judgments. Didn't matter that she was now a fifty-four-year-old tenured professor at one of the finest universities on the West Coast, with two doctorates under her belt. When she came back to La Pierre, at one point or another, she reverted back to that shame-filled little girl without a daddy.

"So you're Clyde's, then?" he asked, frowning.

"No," she snapped coldly, not qualifying her answer this time.

"Criminy, Pete, get off the woman's back already," the bartender said, rifling through her apron pockets. "I'm sure she's had a hard day already and doesn't need you grilling her like a T-bone right now. Here," she said, handing him a wrinkled dollar bill. "Go put something happy on the jukebox, would you?"

Lena met the other woman's gaze and mouthed a furtive *"thank you"*. She hadn't taken the time to notice before, but the woman looked faintly familiar.

"Ruthie Fontaine," the bartender supplied with a smile. "We were in high school together before you..." She trailed off, picked up a white rag, and began to wipe down the well-worn bar top.

Ruthie Fontaine.

Lena cast her memory back and tugged out the cobweb-covered image of a young girl with golden hair, bright eyes and a quick smile, just a year ahead of Lena.

"I remember, now. You were valedictorian," she recalled out loud before she could stop herself. She was usually pretty good in social situations, but reminding Ruthie of that fact while she was in the middle of a Tuesday shift at a crummy bar in the same dead end town they'd both grown up in had surely been a misstep.

Ruthie's golden hair had faded to the color of dishwater, but her smile was as quick and easy as Lena remembered.

"Yeah, I was kind of a big deal back then. That and a buck will buy me a coke," she shot back, tossing the rag into the sink beside her. "Seriously, though, I had considered trying to work for NASA but then decided it would be way better for myself and future generations of Fontaines if I got knocked up my first semester at college, came home with my tail between my legs, and lived in my parents' garage for ten years. Lucky thing, too, because otherwise I wouldn't have all this." She raised both hands to gesture around the bar, her wry grin still firmly in place and holding barely a trace of bitterness. "I've used my big old brain and done the math. By my calculations, I should be able to retire by the time I'm ninety-six, so...living the dream."

Lena was surprised to find that the tension after her awkward gaffe was gone and she was smiling back at Ruthie, her mood lifting a little. "Well, I think you made an excellent decision. It's not like you can get endless, bottom-shelf gin and free pickled eggs at Yale, am I right?"

Ruthie let out a guffaw that was so genuine, it made Lena chuckle in response. This was good. Exactly what she'd needed. A few minutes to shut her brain off and not think about Maeve's death or the sticky mess that awaited her back at Blanchard Manor.

Lena was about to ask Ruthie if she was allowed to have a drink on the job when the strains of a familiar tune poured from the jukebox, forcing a groan from the other woman.

"Seriously, Pete?" Ruthie shouted across the room. "I said a happy song, for crying out loud."

It was only when the violin kicked in that Lena recognized the melody.

Dust in the Wind.

Perfect.

Get the rest of Maeve's Girls, out now and free in KU!

Made in the USA
Columbia, SC
17 March 2023